Cats and Dogs

Mrs. Brody click-click-clicked into the kitchen. When she was gone, Lou pointed an accusing paw at the kitten.

"I'm on to you, *kitty*," he said, "and you're in big trouble. *Grrrrrrr*."

The kitten's big, sweet eyes suddenly went slitty and venomous. His squeaky little meow morphed into the throaty, Russian-accented growl of a full-grown male feline agent.

"I sink not, baby puppy!" the kitten said. "Eet ees you who ees in trouble."

Cats and Dogs

by Elizabeth Lenhard

Scholastic Ltd.

New York ~ Toronto ~ London ~ Auckland ~ Sydney
Mexico City ~ New Delhi ~ Hong Kong ~ Buenos Aires

Scholastic Children's Books,
Commonwealth House, 1-19 New Oxford Street,
London WC1A 1NU
A division of Scholastic Ltd.
London ~ New York ~ Toronto ~ Auckland
Mexico City ~ New Delhi ~ Hong Kong ~ Buenos Aires

First published in the USA by Scholastic Inc., New York 2001
This edition published in the UK by Scholastic Ltd., 2001

ISBN 0 439 97921 8

Design by Louise Bova

10 9 8 7 6 5 4 3 2 1

Printed by Bath Press, England

For Adam

Contents

Contents

Cats and Dogs

Chapter One

It was an ordinary spring evening. Kids were out playing. Mums were bringing home the bacon. And dogs around the world were watching a developing story on CNN, the Canine News Network.

A shaggy-faced, pointy-eared newscaster addressed the camera, looking grim.

"This is Wolf Blitzer," the wolf said. He held a microphone in one paw and a page of notes in the other. "We have breaking news from Sector C-47."

The image cut away to a pretty white house with a wraparound porch, a blue front door, and a boy on the front lawn. The kid had big trainers and a floppy brown fringe. He was dribbling a soccer ball around the grass when a white four-wheel-drive vehicle pulled into the driveway and a smartly dressed woman hopped out.

Wolf ruffled his papers. "At approximately 3:32 P.M. today, Mrs. Brody arrived home with groceries and in a development that has confounded World

1

Council analysts, she failed to notice a tabby cat playing with a ball of yarn in the front yard."

A shaky paw-held camera focused on Mrs. Brody reaching into the rear hatch of the four-wheel-drive and pulling out some brown paper bags.

Wolf continued. "Scotty Brody, age eleven, was also oblivious to this sinister invasion. Even the alarm signal of our agent on the scene, known to his humans as 'Buddy', didn't alert the Brodys."

The camera swerved to catch a cute, grey-striped cat romping in the front yard. Then the shot zoomed into a front window of the house, where a droopy-eyed bloodhound was barking so hard that his long floppy ears flapped in the air.

The camera swerved back to the front door as Scott Brody walked through it.

"Calm down, Buddy," he called. "It's just me. It's okay, we're home . . . Buddy . . . *wait!*"

The paw held camera gave a jolt as Buddy tore out of the house.

"*MROOOOWRR!*" the tabby screeched, darting down the street.

"As you'd expect, our agent pounced at the intruder at his first opportunity," Wolf Blitzer read. "A dramatic high-speed chase ensued. Our exclusive Bloodhound-Cam – mounted in one of Buddy's fangs – caught the action. Our sports announcer, Bob Bouvier, will give us the play-by-play. Bob?"

The head of a mammoth woolly grey dog filled the screen.

"Thanks, Wolf," Bob said quickly. "Well, folks, this spine-tingling chase began with the old cat-up-the-tree trick . . ."

The wobbling Bloodhound-Cam raced after the tabby as the evil cat scrambled up a spindly tree.

Boom!

"Oooh, Buddy hit that tree *hard*. But he recovered quickly. In fact, he's tried to climb after the evil cat. *But the tree couldn't hold him.* It bent to the ground – the cat was within Buddy's reach! But no, it wasn't meant to be!"

The skinny tree, with the cat scowling in its branches, slipped from the dog's grip. The trunk snapped upright, taking the tabby with it.

"*Mrrroooowwwrr!*" the feline screeched as he flew through the air.

The Bloodhound-Cam gave chase, galloping into the kitchen of a nearby house. Buddy arrived just in time to see the cat fly through the window and collide with a grey-haired woman lifting a pie from the oven.

"Aaaaaaah!" the woman screamed. As the cat knocked her across the room, the pie hit the ceiling with a *splat*. Then the cat darted away.

"Our agent will not be shaken," Bob narrated excitedly. "As you can see, he chased the evil feline through the living room and up the stairs. Okay, here, the bloodhound hit a snag – the classic bunched-up carpet gag got him running in place! But he recovered quickly to chase the cat back *down* the stairs. Let's see what Buddy will do next in this blood-pumping

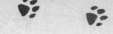

pursuit . . . Okay, he headed for the sliding glass door, but it wasn't open and – OH! That's *gotta* hurt."

The Bloodhound-Cam slid slowly down the glass door.

"Looks like Buddy needs to study up on his Chase Tactics 101 text," Bob quipped.

On the other side of the door, the tabby cackled and pointed at Buddy tauntingly before running off.

"*That* was a definite setback," Bob admitted. "But look, our agent is on the prowl again. He's on the pavement. And . . . what's that on the Bloodhound-Cam? The cat's in the street. It looks like he's been hit. The tabby is down – I repeat, *the tabby is down*."

The Bloodhound-Cam crept towards the cat, wobbling slightly as Buddy sniffed at the feline.

And that was when the tabby's yellow eyes popped open. He flashed an evil grin and swiped at Buddy's nose with glinting claws. Then he darted out of the street.

After that, the screen filled with chaos – thunderous barking, a firing motor, and a screech of tyres. The Bloodhound-Cam swerved and caught – a rusty brown van careering down on Buddy!

Screeeeech! Thud!

The camera fell sideways and remained still. But it did manage to capture the van speeding away. Peeking out of the back window was the sneering face of a calico cat.

The picture went dead with a *zzzzzttt*.

Back on the live feed, Wolf Blitzer appeared again, looking shaken.

"One of our best agents," he said, "taken down in the line of duty. May Buddy rest in peace."

The newscaster flicked a tear from his eye with a long, sharp claw and took a deep breath.

"Naturally, the World Dog Council has taken swift action. Our WDC correspondent, Susie Chow, is on location to fill us in on the latest. Susie?"

The image cut to a beautifully coiffed dog with a blue-black tongue. Clutching her microphone, she stood on a busy pavement next to a fire hydrant.

"Wolf," Susie said, "I'm standing outside the entrance to the famous World Dog Council. Inside, a flurry of activity is taking place to deal with what's come to be known as 'The Brody Brouhaha'."

The camera cut to a bustling military control room filled with dogs. Dogs were barking into headsets. Dogs were typing on computers. A cluster of dogs hovered around a slobbery mastiff with five gold stars on his collar. Their paws were drawn up in stiff salutes.

"That's General Charles, chief military officer," Susie whispered. "After the council received word of Buddy's death, the general issued his orders."

The camera zoomed in on the mastiff's glistening mouth.

"My God," he yelled, spraying his subordinates with spit. "Get the best darn agent you can in there. ASAP!"

The broadcast cut to another paw-held camera

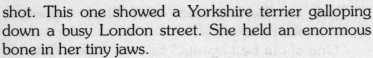

shot. This one showed a Yorkshire terrier galloping down a busy London street. She held an enormous bone in her tiny jaws.

"The directive was sent by bone messenger to one Sergeant Rott," Susie narrated. "Rott, of course, heads up the Dog Council's elite training corps."

The Yorkie reached a quiet London park. She trotted casually down a path until she reached a massive rottweiler, who was pretending to sniff a lamppost.

"And here they make the exchange," Susie said.

The Yorkie dropped the bone. Immediately, the rottweiler snatched it up and ducked beneath a nearby bush. The camera followed, capturing the rottweiler as he bit the hollow "bone" in half. Inside was a scroll of paper and a photograph of Mrs. Brody, standing in front of a real estate sign that said "SOLD"!

"With that, the rottweiler took off, literally," Susie said. "He caught the first cargo flight out of Heathrow Airport. Wolf, he is en route to America as we speak. And with him is a fresh litter of replacement agents – English setter puppies, fresh from the academy. And very cute indeed."

The paw-held camera captured the rottweiler sitting to attention in the cargo hold of an airplane. He was surrounded by trunks and suitcases. And at his feet sat a line of serious-looking puppies, their fur trimmed into military buzz cuts.

Susie appeared on camera again.

"If all goes according to plan, a new agent will be

in place by morning. And the world may, I repeat, *may* be safe for another day. I'm Susie Chow, Canine News Network. Back to you, Wolf."

Chapter Two

*L*ittermate number 4 heaved a weary sigh and glared at his fellow foxhounds. The plump little dogs were yipping and yapping their way through a game of tag.

How can these, these . . . *puppies* be my brothers and sisters? he wondered. Yes, they looked exactly like him – they had the same stocky white legs and floppy brown ears and wagging, white-tipped tails. And just like him, they had been born in this old barn stall three months earlier.

But there the similarity ended.

"How can they just *play* like there's nothing wrong?" littermate number 4 muttered. "Don't they know we're trapped here? This stall is no better than a jail! I don't care how warm and comfy it is."

The foxhound stuck out his fuzzy chest. He'd had enough of these baby games. He was going to see the world. Yes, he – littermate number 4 – had a plan!

He stalked through the tangle of puppies, batting

at wiggling tails with his nose.

"Outta the way," he barked. "Clear the area!"

Number 4's older sister (by 2½ minutes) rolled her brown eyes and growled at him.

"Not again!" she complained. "What is it this time?"

Number 4 pointed to a pitchfork lying on a bale of hay. The fork's handle hung off the end of the bale.

With a few yips and growls, number 4 climbed up the enormous block of hay and plopped into the cradle of the sharp fork. He pointed a white paw at a rope dangling in front of his snout. Then he pointed up. The other end of the rope was tied around another hay bale dangling from a ceiling beam. And that hay bale was positioned just over the pitchfork's handle.

"When I pull this rope," littermate number 4 boasted, "the hay is gonna fall on the pitchfork and send me soaring over the stall wall and on to freedom! So step back!"

Before number 4 could get a grip on the rope, one of his siblings spoke up.

"What is it with you?" he yapped.

"Me?" number 4 said. "What's with you? I want adventure! I don't want to wait for someone to take me to some boring old house."

"What's wrong with that?" asked number 2. "A family that loves you. Not to mention free food, a warm place to sleep . . ."

"And you can go to the bathroom wherever you

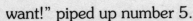

want!" piped up number 5.

"*Growrrrrrrr,*" sighed the puppies longingly.

Number 4 barked impatiently.

"Don't you want to do something exciting?" he demanded. "Like be a police dog or one of those Russian space dogs? Maybe sample the great bones of Europe?"

His siblings panted and looked at him blankly.

"Oh, forget it," the puppy growled. Then he gazed over the stall wall. Who knew what lay beyond?

"World, here I come!" he announced.

Littermate number 4 gripped the rope in his teeth and gave it a yank. The bale of hay came loose with a jerk and plummeted towards the pitchfork handle. It was a direct hit! The pitchfork flung forward and sent number 4 flying, up, up and awa—

"*Arf!*"

Splat!

The foxhound shook his head blearily. Hay . . . he saw nothing but hay. He squirmed and snuffled out of the pile of straw. And there – he found himself nose to nose with his oldest brother, number 1.

"Back from your adventure so soon, Scooby Doofus?!" the puppy taunted.

"*Arf, arf, arf,*" his sibs giggled.

With a sinking heart, number 4 realized he had hit the wall and bounced right back into his puppy prison. His ears sagged and he flopped back into the pile of straw. *What* a bummer.

Bzzzzzzzzz.

Huh?

Number 4 watched the other puppies scramble as a lethal round saw blade broke through the barn floor! In an instant, the blade had cut a perfect circle out of the floor. And through that circle poked the big, boxy, brown-and-black head of a rottweiler. The massive dog leaped into the stall and barked at the puppies.

"Into the hole," he ordered. "Into the hole!"

Number 4 gasped as the rottweiler began grabbing his brothers and sisters by the scruff of their necks and tossing them down the chute. The puppy burrowed deeper into his pile of straw.

When he peeked back out, his siblings had all disappeared. And now the rottweiler was peering into the hole.

"Front and centre," he growled. "Up, up, up!"

Five teenage puppies with short tan fur and spindly legs scampered into the stall. They formed a straight line at the rottweiler's paws.

"Who are they?" number 4 murmured to himself.

"Agents!" the rottweiler barked.

"Oh," number 4 whispered in awe.

"You wanted excitement?!" the rottweiler yelled at the new puppies. "You wanted adventure? Well, here it is! You are the best of the best. Now – are you ready?"

"Sir, yes, sir!" the puppies barked.

"Good luck," the big dog said gruffly. "And look cute!" Then he dived through the hole and disappeared.

Just in time, too. Here came the farmer – the guy

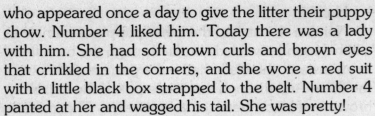

who appeared once a day to give the litter their puppy chow. Number 4 liked him. Today there was a lady with him. She had soft brown curls and brown eyes that crinkled in the corners, and she wore a red suit with a little black box strapped to the belt. Number 4 panted at her and wagged his tail. She was pretty!

"Oooh," said the lady, smiling down at number 4.

"Whoa," said the farmer, scratching his head and gaping at the replacement puppies. "They've really grown fast . . . and changed colour . . . and . . . breed?"

Suddenly number 4 was swooping upwards. The lady had scooped him into her arms. She tickled his ears and cooed, "He's *adorable*."

"Well, Mrs. Brody," said the farmer, "I guess he's yours then."

The next thing number 4 knew, he'd been tossed into a brown box with a few holes cut in the sides. Then he was bouncing around the back seat of a car. A real car! Number 4 had seen cars through the cracks in the barn wall, but he'd never dreamed he'd get to ride in one some day.

"The rottweiler was right," number 4 whispered. "My adventure has begun!"

Bounce. Bounce. Bounce.

Littermate number 4 was rolling crazily around his cardboard box as Mrs. Brody strode away from the car in her clicking, high-heeled shoes. Finally, the foxhound got a grip on the cardboard so he could peek out of one of the holes. He spied a pretty white house with a wraparound porch covered with flowerpots. Now they were going through the blue front door.

Mrs. Brody walked down a hallway to a big, funny-looking metal door with locks and bolts all over it. A red light flashed above it. She banged on the door with her fist.

Crash!

Number 4 cocked his ears to the sound of breaking glass and splashing liquid.

"Oh – ouch!" yelled a muffled voice from behind the door. "Coming!"

Then Mrs. Brody *click-click-clicked* into the kitchen. She plunked number 4's box onto the counter and called, "Hi, sweetheart."

Sweetheart! Who's that? Number 4 peeked through a different hole and spied a kid – a boy – sprawled on a couch in the family room, watching soccer on TV and doing homework at the same time.

"*Arf!*" Number 4 yipped happily. Boys were the best kind of humans. At least that's what he'd heard through the puppy grapevine.

"I've got a surprise for you, Scott," Mrs. Brody sang to her son. Then light filled number 4's box and her hand dipped in to scoop him up.

"A new puppy!" Mrs. Brody announced.

Number 4 saw the boy's face fall.

"But, Mom," he said, "it's only been a week since Buddy died!"

"I'm sorry, honey," Mrs. Brody replied. "I know

13

it's a bit soon. But he's very sweet."

The foxhound gave her a thank-you lick on the thumb.

"So?" Scott pouted.

Uh-oh, number 4 thought. This doesn't look good.

"So, look at him," Mrs. Brody exclaimed, snuggling number 4. "He's adorable. And smart. And just the right size. You could teach him tricks, play catch or Frisbee . . ."

Scott glowered at his mother, and Mrs. Brody's bright smile quickly faded.

"This isn't working at all, is it?" she asked her son.

"Mom, I'm eleven now, okay?" Scott scoffed.

"And so *very* wise," Mrs. Brody joked, giving him a poke in the ribs. "Anyway, your father needs him for his work in the lab, so maybe you could just be nice?"

Slam!

Littermate number 4 jumped as the metal door in the hallway flew open. That must be The Lab, he thought. He craned his neck. A very tall, very skinny man with a mop of crazy black curls and really thick glasses was quickly stumbling towards him. He swiped number 4 out of Mrs. Brody's hand and squinted at him.

"Ah, yes, perfect," Professor Brody murmured, poking at number 4's belly and tickling his chin.

"Arf, arf, arffffff," number 4 giggled.

"Mm-hm, retinal response normal," the man said, peering into number 4's eyes. "Standard dander composition. Immune response . . ."

The professor buried his nose in number 4's soft belly and took a deep breath. Then the man's enormous nostrils began to flare and flutter and twitch.

"*Aaaaachooo!*" the professor sneezed, showering number 4 with spit. Then, without so much as an "excuse me," he thunked the puppy down in front of Scott and dashed back to the lab, muttering, "Excellent!"

Whew, what a weirdo, number 4 thought. Oops, here he comes again.

The professor shot back into the kitchen.

"Sorry, forgot my family duties again, didn't I," he said with a nervous laugh. He planted a kiss on Mrs. Brody's cheek.

"Honey," he said.

He patted Scott on the head.

"Son," he said.

And then . . . there was an awkward silence.

Oh, brother, number 4 thought, even puppies have better communication skills than this. He watched the professor point at Scott's homework.

"Oh, mathematics!" the man exclaimed. "Uh . . . well, um, when you get to algebra, have I got a funny story for you. Ah, sigma . . ."

Professor Brody's eyes glazed over. His family forgotten again, he wandered back to the lab, chortling.

The door slammed shut. Scott scowled. Mrs. Brody cringed and scooped up number 4 again, holding him out to Scott.

"Why don't you name him?" she said.

Scott kicked at a chair leg with his trainer.

"Ask Dad," he sneered. "It's his dog . . ."

"He's *our* dog," Mrs. Brody said. "Now why don't you give him a name."

"Okay," Scott replied. "How about Loser?"

Hey, number 4 thought. No need to be insulting! *Beep-beep-beep-beep.*

That black box hooked to Mrs. Brody's belt was making a ton of noise. She grabbed it and peered at a little screen on its face.

"Oh! The open house!" she remembered. "I have to go."

She cuddled number 4 some more and kissed his nose. Then she crooned to him, "But you're not a loser, are you? No, you're not . . . hey, wait. *Lou.* We'll call you Lou."

She looked number 4 in the eyes and declared, "Your name is Lou."

"Zer," Scott muttered. Mrs. Brody didn't hear him, but of course the puppy's sensitive ears picked it up. He looked at Scott and stuck his tongue out at him. Then he turned his new name over in his mind. Lou, he thought. LOU. Loooouuu. He loved it!

Suddenly Lou found himself on the kitchen floor. And Mrs. Brody was click-click-clicking out of the room.

"Be good, boys," she called to Lou and Scott. "But no playing in the living room. That rug is Uzbekistani, ten thousand thread count."

In an instant, she was gone, and Lou was alone with Scott. Scott – a big-footed boy who didn't like him.

Scott felt Lou staring at him. He glared down at the little foxhound.

"What?" he demanded.

Lou stared some more. Scott huffed in annoyance and picked Lou up. He carried Lou through a sliding glass door and plopped him onto the back porch.

"Go dig up the yard or something," Scott ordered. He slid the glass door shut and stomped away.

Lou peered after him, smearing his nose on the glass.

"Huh," he said. "Must be a cat person."

Then he shrugged his fuzzy shoulders and turned around. He gasped. The back yard – it was huge! And it was Lou's, all Lou's! There was even a red kennel! With a yip of joy, the newly named puppy scampered down the steps.

It was time to explore.

Chapter Three

*L*ou darted happily across the neatly mowed grass. A dandelion! He sniffed the weed happily. Oooh! A worm! Lou was just getting ready to examine the critter when a fabulous scent distracted him.

"Ahhh," he whispered, sniffing the air. "Puppy food!" He looked up and gasped. Dangling from a silver balloon, a dog biscuit floated down into the back yard. Gently, the cookie landed at Lou's feet.

Lou sniffed it eagerly. Mmmmm, liver flavour! he thought. My favourite! He opened his mouth wide and prepared to gobble. That was when a rumbling, grumbling voice stopped him in midbite.

"I wouldn't do that if I were you."

Lou yipped in surprise and whirled around. A grizzled chocolate labrador with a grey snout and tired, saggy brown eyes stared him down. Lou was about to say hello when he remembered something. Hey, this is *my* back yard, Lou thought. That ol' dog is *on my turf*!

"*Grrrrrr,*" Lou growled.

The big lab merely laughed dryly. "I like your spirit, kid," he said. "But you oughta stand back."

Then he kicked a twig at Lou's cookie.

"Hey," the puppy squeaked. "That's my bis—"
POW!

"Whoa!" Lou blinked at the spot where his biscuit had been. Now it was just a circle of charred grass. The cookie had exploded to smithereens.

"That could have been my head!" Lou whispered, trembling.

"And that would have been the shortest assignment in history," the old dog said. "I guess HQ ain't training you guys the way they used to."

Huh? Lou stared at the old dog in confusion.

"Name's Butch," the lab said gruffly, sticking out his paw to shake. "What kind of stupid name did the bipeds saddle *you* with? Spot? Fifi? Rover?"

"Lou," Lou said.

"God forbid," grumbled Butch. "Oh! *Lou.* Sorry."

Lou glanced at the Brody house. "Is that boy always so grumpy?" he asked. "Maybe they should switch his food."

"Humans can be a little emotional. You'll get used to it," Butch said. Then he headed toward Lou's red kennel. "Come on . . ."

"Uh . . ." Lou said as he followed the dog nervously, "who exactly are y— ?"

"Save the questions for after the briefing," Butch grunted. Then he ducked into the kennel. Lou followed him and gazed at the bare, rough, wooden walls. What were they doing in here?

Butch swatted at a bent nail sticking out of the wall. Lou gaped as the shabby wood zipped away. Behind it was a glowing blue TV screen! It was surrounded by speakers, buttons, switches and a bowl of doggy treats.

"Coooool!" Lou gasped.

"Standard equipment," Butch said as he busied himself with some buttons. "You got your EC-3 videophone, research archive database, cipher charts, Snausages, et cetera . . ."

Lou fixed his eyes on a pretty blue button and reached for it.

"Heel!" Butch barked.

"*Yip,*" Lou squeaked, yanking his paw away.

"That's the Big Button," Butch yelled, shaking his jowls at Lou. "You don't just *press* the Big Button. Jeez!"

"Sorry . . ." Lou said, his tail between his legs.

"Just try to remember your training," the lab grunted. "Now, let's get started."

Butch flipped a switch with his nose. A picture filled the screen. It looked like an ID card. In the corner was a photo of a saggy-eared bloodhound.

"This was the Brodys' last dog, Agent 349L6, aka Buddy," Butch explained. "Last week he was hit by a car. Assassinated."

"But he looks like such a nice dog," Lou said, gazing sadly at the picture. Butch gave him a curious glance. Then he hit the bent nail again. The video screen zinged away as quickly as it had appeared.

"That is too cool," Lou breathed as he scampered out of the kennel behind Butch. The lab was heading to the wooden fence that enclosed the back yard.

Butch stood in front of one of the fence planks.

Whooosh.

In an instant, the plank disappeared.

"Wow!" Lou yelled. He poked his head through the opening to see an alley filled with garages and garbage cans. Freedom!

"All right, agent," Butch said, stepping through the opening. "Let's meet the team."

"Agent!" Lou whispered with a grin. He followed the big dog through the fence. When Lou landed in the alley, Butch turned back to the fence.

"Can't forget to lock up," he said. Then he pressed his paw onto a knothole on the outside of the fence. The brown circle began to glow. Then it turned green. It pulsed beneath Butch's paw and the fence plank whooshed shut.

Butch ignored Lou's gasps of amazement and trotted over to a row of dustbins. They were leaning against the house next door.

"Kid, look over there," Butch ordered, pointing with his nose at the bins. "That's Peek."

"Oh . . . kay . . ." Lou said. He stared hard at the bins but saw no one.

Butch shook his head and pressed his paw to a little silver button in his collar.

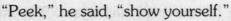

"Peek," he said, "show yourself."

With a mechanical hum, one of the dustbins rose from the ground. Beneath it was a glowing plastic cylinder, filled with computers, screens, periscopes . . . and one very funny-looking dog. Peek was a Chinese crested. His whole body was shaved except for some wild tan tendrils sticking out of his head.

"Peek's early warning," Butch explained. "He's got radar, sonar, thermo-imaging and odour matrixing. He can detect any non-residential cat in a three-block radius."

"Hey, guys," Peek said in a squeaky good-fella voice. He gave Lou a wave. Lou gaped.

"Peek, fall in," Butch ordered. The funny little dog hopped out of his radar hut and trotted along behind Butch and Lou. They walked down the alley towards the pavement. Then Butch hit the button on his collar again.

"Sam?" he said. "What's your location?"

A huffing, puffing voice echoed through the alley. Lou looked around wildly. Then he realised the voice was coming out of Butch's collar! It was a two-way radio!

"I'm one-eighteenth of a klick east," the voice said. "I'm gonna backtrack using a standard delta approach in three, two, one . . ."

Suddenly Sam – a big, fat, woolly English sheepdog with too-long a fringe – burst into the alley. He crashed through some bushes and crept, spylike, along the ground until he sat in front of Butch and saluted.

"Request permission to pant heavily, sir," Sam barked.

"Granted," Butch said.

"*Huh-uh-huh-uh-huh* . . ." Sam panted, slobbering heavily. Butch led the three dogs onto the pavement and slapped a heavy paw onto Lou's shoulder.

"Boys," he grunted at Peek and Sam, "I want you to meet, ahem, Lou. He's fresh from the academy and he's—"

"Human!" Peek warned. A man with a briefcase was walking down the street. Lou watched as the other dogs wagged their tails and scampered about like, well, normal dogs. Sam even ran over to a neighbour's driveway and scooped a newspaper into his mouth.

When the man was out of sight, Sam spat the paper out.

"*Blech!*"

Butch glanced around to make sure no one else was coming.

"All right, kid," Butch said. "We don't have much time. Here's the low-down . . ."

Lou tried hard to listen, really he did. But he hadn't had any playtime for an entire hour, and his tail was so enticing. Lou gave up and started chasing his tail while Butch was speaking.

Whee! No matter how hard he chased, he couldn't catch that darn tail! Whee!

As he chased, Lou was dimly aware of Butch's voice.

"Your new master, the professor, loves dogs – but he's allergic. And for a few ye— Holy dog droppings!" Butch growled.

Uh-oh. Lou looked up from his blissful playing to see Butch glowering at him.

"Come with me!" the lab ordered. Lou, Sam and Peek followed Butch back through the fence and to the kennel. While the dog turned on the videophone, Lou, Sam and Peek hovered outside the door. Lou listened nervously. He saw a long-nosed collie wearing headphones appear on the screen.

"You promised me a professional!" Butch roared at the collie. "And what do I get? A puppy! A wet-behind-the-ears, ordinary puppy! This kid's never *heard* of the academy, much less been there!"

"It was an accident," the collie said. "He slipped through. But things are moving too fast. The cat envoy officially denies any involvement and our intelligence verifies it. Top Dog thinks this one's definitely a rogue."

"So," Butch replied, "let's get rid of the puppy . . ."

While Butch paused to give his ear a scratch, Lou gasped. Get rid of the puppy! No!

"There's no time," he heard the collie say.

Yes! Lou thought.

The collie continued: "The professor's almost finished, and if the rest of your team does its job, there shouldn't be a problem. Out."

The collie disappeared from the screen.

"*Grrrrr,*" Butch grumbled again.

"Yay!" Lou cried, doing a somersault.

"I think that if I'm gonna be a secret agent, I should have a better name. I was thinking 'Toto Annihilation'."

"Nah," Peek said, "he's a pro wrestler."

"All right, then, 'Doom Machine'."

Butch stalked out of the kennel and barked at Lou.

"You can call yourself Squicky the Space Dog for all I care," Butch grumbled. "But that don't make your behind a rocket pack. You are *not* an agent, but you *are* gonna help us. So first things first. Come with me."

Lou and the other dogs followed Butch back into the kennel. While Sam peeked in through the door, Peek plopped himself behind a computer keyboard.

Butch glowered down at Lou and announced, "History 101. Dogs have always been man's best friend. I'm sure even you know that," he said.

Lou nodded.

"But cats," Butch hissed, "they're another story. Peek, start with ancient Egypt."

"Oh, like we haven't seen *that* five billion times," Peek complained, swiping a paw through the bobbling tendrils of fur on his head. "Why don't we ju—"

"*Grrrrrrr,*" Butch growled.

"So okay, okay, never mind," Peek squeaked. "Here goes."

He flicked a few keys on his keyboard and the screen came alive. Lou saw a bunch of squiggles drawn on a wall. There were also pictures of pyramids and funny-looking humans with cats at their feet.

"See these?" Butch asked, pointing at the squiggles. "A human will read these hieroglyphics and tell you that ancient people *worshipped* cats. But in reality, they were *ruled* by them."

The video screen showed cartoon cats whipping the backs of humans shoving giant bricks along the ground.

"Some evil cat named Shen-Akh-Akumon – he forced them to build pyramids and monuments and generally treated them like they were his litter box," Butch said. "Things were terrible."

"Oooh," Sam panted, "this is the best part. *Uh-huh-uh-huh-uh-huh.*"

"So the dogs," Butch continued, "being man's best friend, rose up and put the cats down. And with humans back on top, we just took our natural place at their side."

"And people just forgot?" Lou asked.

"You have to remember," Peek said as he typed on the keyboard, "humans are a *very* primitive species. They can't sense earthquakes, they can't smell fear. Heck, they can't even take responsibility for their own farts."

Butch nodded sagely. He continued his history lesson as they walked out of the kennel.

"To cut a long story short," Butch said, heading back to the fence, "Professor Brody is allergic to dogs and he's obsessed with finding the cure."

"We think he's almost done," Peek piped up.

"But our guess," Butch said with a scowl, "is that

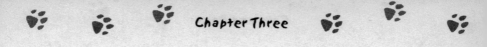

the cats want to steal the formula and adapt it to cure cat allergies instead. If that happens, the balance of power shifts back to them."

"For three thousand years, cats have been waiting for a moment like this," Sam blustered. "Waiting to get a leg up on us dogs and regain control of the planet!"

"Eh, don't be melodramatic," said Peek. "It'll never get that far." The fence plank whooshed open and he stepped into the alley. Sam and Butch followed, but before the fence closed again, Butch poked his head through the opening.

"So the mission is this," he said, looking Lou in the eye. "Keep the cats away from the professor's lab until he finishes the formula. Got it?"

"Yes, sir," Lou said. He tried to sound more confident than he felt.

Butch nodded at him sceptically. He sighed and rummaged beneath a bush near the fence. He dug up a dog collar that he slipped over Lou's head, tightening it to fit his little neck.

"This collar was Buddy's," Butch said roughly. "It's yours now. And remember, you're the last line of defence. See anything weird, just call on your collar."

"Yes, sir," Lou squeaked. "I just have one question. What's ancient Egypt?"

"Argh!" Butch rolled his eyes as he slapped a paw on the knothole and the fence plank whooshed closed.

Lou blinked hard for a few moments. Then he began to feel a bit giddy. And then . . . he started to giggle!

He curled his lip into a scowl and raised the fur on his back.

"Freeze, cat!" he barked. "I'm an agent!"

He karate-chopped the air with his paw.

"Ha-*ha*! Whack!" he yipped. "I'm an agent! Hi-*yah*. Take that! And th—"

"There you are!"

"*Arp!*" Lou yelped. He spun around to find himself gazing up, up, up at the frazzled Professor Brody.

"Easy," the professor said. "It's just me. Now stay."

Lou sat obediently and watched the professor take something out of his lab coat pocket. It was a big, long . . . vaccination needle. Agent or no, Lou couldn't help but whine in protest. Please, not the shot, he thought desperately.

The professor lifted the needle . . .

Anything but the shot! Lou thought. Noooooo!

But the professor plunged the needle into his own arm.

"*Grooooowwww,*" Lou sighed with relief.

Suddenly the professor grabbed him, swooping Lou up towards his nose. And once again, the professor buried his beak into Lou's fur, inhaling deeply.

"Good . . . good . . ." the professor said, grinning.

Then his nostrils began to shudder and flutter and twitch.

"*Achooo!*" the man sneezed. "Darn!"

Lou blinked away another spray of professor spit

and eyed his new owner irritably. Then his eyes widened. What was that bubbly spot erupting on the professor's hand? It was . . . it was green! And there was one on his cheek! And another. And another!

"OH!" the professor shrieked. He dropped Lou and raced to the back door. He ran inside just as Scott was coming out, carrying a black-and-white ball.

"Hey, Dad," Scott said, "you wanna help me practise for soccer tryouts?"

"Maybe later!" the green-and-spotty professor shouted as he ran to his lab. "I need to lance a few things."

Scott scowled and walked back into the house. He slid the glass door shut, leaving Agent "Doom Machine" Lou to think about his wild, wonderful day.

He couldn't believe it! He, little littermate number 4, was a powerful doggy agent with the weight of dogdom on his shoulders!

And he had his very own boy, even if the boy didn't like him.

And on his very first day in the big wide world, he had evaded the dog biscuit of death! Not bad for a new recruit. Not bad at all.

Chapter Four

I can't believe it, thought Calico the cat. That little squirt evaded the dog biscuit of death.

Calico shuddered. He glanced at his compadres – the minklike Havana brown, the ruthless, no-tail Manx, the muscle-bound Burmese. They were all sitting on top of a long, majestic dining room table. Which was inside a long, majestic dining room. Which lay deep in the enormous hilltop mansion of their leader, the Great Persian. Calico was hoping the other cats would look as nervous as he felt. But no, they were completely cool and confident. The tabby was even purring!

Darn smug purebreds, Calico thought. It's so easy for them. Me, I'm just a common American shorthair. It's a miracle that I even made it into the Great Persian's inner circle.

Calico began to purr as he remembered the fateful day he met the First Feline at the kitty groomer's. That had been a few months earlier, back when Calico had

had an owner, a simpering little girl who had showered him with hugs and kisses and love – yuck.

At the blow-dry station, the Persian had told Calico about his plan to conquer the world.

"Uh-huh. How're you gonna make all that happen?" the Calico had asked, rolling his green eyes. "What, are you rich or something?"

"Why, yessssss," the Persian had hissed. "I have recently acquired an owner, one Mr. Mason. The man is a billionaire. He's also practically a corpse. I have the run of the house – that is, I and my loyal crew of evil cats. When we have succeeded, the world will be my scratching post. I, the Great Persian, will rule all humans, and more importantly, all dogs, with an iron paw!"

The Persian unleashed a great, wheezing, evil cackle.

This kitty's certifiably crazy, Calico thought. But he's also my ticket out of here!

"Hey, count me in," he said.

Calico's escape from the little girl's arms had been a cinch.

It had been easier still to sneak into the Persian's limousine. And now he lived with the other cats in the nooks and crannies of Mr. Mason's mansion. The house was filled with miles of curtains for slashing and endless furniture for scratching. And the crew's favourite meeting place was this long, shiny dining room table.

The great Persian mounted the table and gazed

twitchily at his kitty brood. As usual, Calico was a bit over-awed by the cat's vicious, smushed-in face; his hateful, slightly crossed eyes, which were the colour of dirty pennies; and his fluffy, fluffy, fluffy white fur. Calico flicked his tail nervously as the great cat began to speak.

"For thousands of years, we have been oppressed," the Persian announced in a high-pitched hiss. "But no more! While our so-called government, pacified by Meow Mix and chicken-flavoured Fancy Feast, does nothing, we will take a giant step forward to reclaim our rightful place as masters of planet Earth!"

"*Mrowr, mrowr, mrowr,*" the cats cheered.

The Persian stalked down the centre of the dining room table, eyeing each of his charges.

"So tell me, one of you," he ordered. "Is the dog out of the way? Did the puppy fall for my clever trap?"

Calico's whiskers trembled. His fellow cats shuffled their paws nervously and gazed at the ceiling.

"None of you have a tale to tell?" the Persian asked. "A little story for me? You!"

The Great One was staring down at Calico.

"Tell me," the Persian demanded, "is the game afoot?"

What game? Calico thought in panic. What foot? Nobody told me about any foot.

"Um, yes?" Calico tried.

"*Why is the game afoot?*" his leader screamed, spitting in rage.

"I, I, I meant . . . no," Calico said.

"Ah, excellent," the Persian purred. "So the puppy is dead. Now we can—"

"Um . . . can I change my answer?" Calico piped.

"*Is the puppy alive or not?!*" the Persian demanded.

"Wellll," Calico said, "another dog told him it was a bomb."

"Another dog," his leader said. "I suspect a professional. But despite this blunder, my devious plot will remain unaffected, will it not?"

"Uhhhhh . . . yes?" Calico said.

Slowly, the Persian's face scrunched into an evil smile.

Calico's fellow cats breathed a sigh of relief and chimed in.

"Oh, yeah!" the Manx agreed.

"Sure!" the Tabby enthused.

"No problem," Calico said. "Project Dark Storm should go down without a hitch."

"Dark Storm," the Persian hissed. "Yes. Because like a powerful dark storm, I will make my presence known to the world. Like a seeping mist, I will creep into the dogs' centre of power and make them quake in fear at the very mention of my name . . ."

"Meeeester Teeenkles!" a high female voice floated through the mansion.

"*Hisssssssss,*" the Persian spat as the other cats tried hard not to giggle.

Yes, it was true. Their evil leader's name was . . .

Mr. Tinkles. And the human calling for him was Sophie, Mr. Mason's plump, cheerful maid. Sophie seemed to spend most of her time searching the mansion for the Persian, calling his name in a thick Italian accent.

"Meeeester Teeeeenkles!"

"*Hide*," the Persian ordered.

Calico and the others dashed beneath the table. They crouched in silence as the dining room door swung open. Sophie's pudgy ankles and sensible shoes padded into the room.

"Oh, Meeeester Teeenkles, there you are!" she cooed at the great leader. "I have been looking all over for you. Where have you been?"

"*Meow*," Mr. Tinkles said sweetly. It was the old "innocent house cat" act.

"Mr. Mason ees going to be so happy to see you," Sophie said. She scooped the Persian into her arms.

"I take you to— ewww! Meeeester Teeenkles, you are a stinky kitty! First, you must have a bath."

"*Mrrrrrrooooowwrr!*" Mr. Tinkles screeched as Sophie carried him out.

"Heh-heh-heh-heh." The cats giggled quietly before slinking out of the dining room.

The cat posse crept down an upstairs hall towards one of the bathrooms. Calico could hear Sophie humming as she plunked the screeching Mr. Tinkles into the tub. Then he heard her scrubbing the Persian thoroughly. Finally, she yanked him out for a brisk towelling.

"*Madonna,*" the maid exclaimed. "I forget your bow. Your pretty bow."

The kitty mob ducked into a linen closet while Sophie bustled down the hall. When the coast was clear, they slithered into the bathroom to join Mr. Tinkles, who looked like a drowned river rat.

"When I rule the earth, that Sophie will be the first to die," the Persian screeched as he dripped on the pink bathmat.

"Heh-heh-heh-heh," Calico giggled.

"There's plenty of room on that list for you!" Mr. Tinkles snapped, turning a venomous yellow eye on Calico.

"Heh . . . ahem," Calico said. "Just clearin' my throat, boss."

"We only have a few days to succeed," Mr. Tinkles said, licking his matted fur angrily. "Although living as a kept beast for the past six months has benefited my ingenious scheme, I cannot stand this humiliation any longer. Am I clear?"

"Uhhh," Calico said, scouring his brain for the right answer.

"Never mind," Mr. Tinkles scowled. His eyes narrowed to malevolent slits.

"The puppy," he announced, "won't survive the night."

Chapter Five

Lou sighed happily. It was the first night of his very important mission! He couldn't wait.

After Mrs. Brody fed him some canned puppy chow – yum! – Lou set out to explore the house. He climbed the stairs and ambled over to Scott's room. The boy lounged on his bed, watching a cartoon on TV and totally ignoring Lou. The puppy sighed and glanced at the TV himself. A dog was beating a cat's head with a mallet, leaving big pink lumps with every whack.

"Heh-heh," Lou giggled to himself. "Dogs rule."

"Time for bed, honey!" said Mrs. Brody, clicking into Scott's bedroom.

"I am in bed," Scott answered.

"Ha-ha," Mrs. Brody said. "Nervous about tryouts tomorrow, huh?"

"No . . ."

"It's okay to be nervous."

"I'm not nervous. I *suck* . . . but I'm not nervous."

Lou had to grin. So did Mrs. Brody. She put a finger to her chin and said, "As a parent, I ask myself, 'Is he saying that because he means it or because he wants me to reassure him?' Hmmm . . ."

She pounced on Scott, tickling him like mad.

"Yes, reassure him," she decided. "You're the most wonderful, bright, special, talented, handsome, well-behaved, sw—"

"Okay, okay," Scott squealed. "Stop!"

Mrs. Brody grinned and sat on the edge of Scott's bed.

"Maybe you should get your father to help you out."

"I'm pretty sure he sucks, too." Lou watched the boy's grin fade away.

"Anyway," Scott said roughly, "he's too busy."

Mrs. Brody bit her lip.

"I'll talk to him," she promised.

"Nah, it's okay."

Mrs. Brody shook her head and gave Scott a kiss on the forehead.

"Get some sleep, honey."

With a determined spring in her step, Scott's mother headed down the stairs. Lou cocked an ear.

"Charles," he heard Mrs. Brody say. "I want to talk to you about Sc— uh . . . the . . . gas bill?"

Lou's tail went limp. How lame! He looked sympathetically at Scott. The boy slumped back on his pillow. He glanced sulkily at Lou.

"What?" he demanded. He rolled his eyes and went back to watching the cartoon.

Lou knew when he wasn't wanted. He slunk out of Scott's room and went downstairs.

A few hours later, after all the humans had gone to sleep, Lou found the little silver button on his collar. He pressed it with his paw.

Krrrrggh, the collar crackled.

"Uh . . . hello?" Lou squeaked. "Sir – uh, Butch?"

Almost instantly, Lou heard Butch's voice grumble out of his collar.

"Kid? That you?!" the lab growled. "What's wrong? Bogeys?"

Lou looked over his shoulder toward Scott's bedroom.

"It's Scott," Lou said. "The boy."

"You mean he's acting funny? Like he's in with the cats? Or maybe he's in disguise. Has he been scratching the furniture or peeing in the potted plants?"

"No, he's just kinda . . . sad," Lou said. "Should I be doing something? Licking? Playing? Looking cuter?"

"No!" Butch barked. "Don't get attached to the kid. He'll just distract you."

"I just felt like I sh—"

"I thought you wanted to be an agent."

"I do," Lou squeaked.

"Well, a good agent keeps his mind on the mission and nothing else."

"Oh, right. Yes, sir." Lou nodded so hard his ears flapped.

He tried really, really hard to follow Butch's order.

Must forget about the boy, he told himself. Even though boys are supposed to be really cool. And even though Scott is clearly upset. Even though I could cheer him up . . . No! I have to think like an agent. An agent with a really tough name. Like . . .

"Um, Butch," Lou said, pressing his collar button one more time. "There's something else. I was wondering – do you think 'Rin Tin Terror' should be my new agent name?"

Lou heard Butch sigh. "Out," he grunted. Before Lou's connection went dead, he heard a voice – a lady's voice – echo from his collar.

"Buuuutttchiiie!" the lady called sadly. "Buuuutchiie, where are you?"

That must be Butch's owner, Lou thought.

"*Grrrr,*" he heard Butch grumble. "Tryin' to save the world and she wants to snuggle!"

Lou took his paw off his collar button so Butch wouldn't hear him giggling. He stalked down the hall and planted himself outside Professor and Mrs. Brody's bedroom.

Time to fulfil my mission! he thought. I'm going to guard the professor all night long. I'm an agent now! No time for sleep.

So Lou guarded. And guarded. And guarded. Fifteen whole minutes must have gone by!

"This is gonna be a long night," Lou whispered through a big yawn. He felt his eyelids start to droop. His nose was just hitting the floor when –

Kkkkrrrrgggh.

"Huh?!" Lou squeaked. "Wha – where?"

"Lou?"

A voice was coming out of his collar.

"It's Peek. I'm picking up a faint signal in there. Maybe just a glitch."

Lou's eyes snapped open.

"I'll go look," he spoke into his collar.

Lou tiptoed down the hall. As quietly as he could, he began to creep down the stairs. He could feel his heart beating hard. *Thud. Thud. Thud.*

So far, he saw nothing.

He crept into the kitchen. Only a little light was on over the sink. Trembling, Lou peeked around chairs and counters. He pushed his collar button.

"Hello, Peek?" Lou said. "Seems clear."

"Probably just a squirrel or something," Peek said. "I'll just let Butch—"

"Kid!"

"Yip!" Lou looked up to see Butch scratching at the sliding glass door and barking at him. His brown eyes were wide with alarm, and was that . . . fear?

Then Butch shouted something that chilled Lou right down to his puppy bones.

"Behind you!"

Chapter Six

*L*ou spun around and found himself gazing at not one but two sinuous, hissing – cats!

Siamese cats, Lou realized with a gasp. Everybody knew those were the most devious, slithery animals in all of catdom.

Trembling, Lou backed away from their squinty blue eyes, their snaky brown tails, their glinting long...

Claws! Razor-sharp claws! They were coming right at him!

"*Arf!*" Lou ducked at exactly the right moment. The cats missed him by a millimetre. Instead, they slashed each other across their twitchy black noses.

But they didn't even meow in pain. They simply began to stalk towards Lou.

"Ooooh," Lou squeaked, and stumbled backwards.

The cats licked their whiskers. They were getting closer . . . and closer . . .

"What do I do?" Lou shouted.

"Bite 'em!" Butch ordered through his collar.

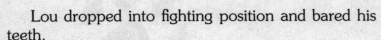

Lou dropped into fighting position and bared his teeth.

"*Grrrrrrrr!*"

That'll scare 'em, he thought.

The cats cackled.

Or . . . maybe not.

Suddenly the Siamese swooped their hind legs around in flawless kung fu circle kicks. Two brown paws caught Lou right in the belly.

"*Aaaaaarrrf,*" he squealed as he flew across the kitchen.

Clang!

The puppy collided with a metal dustbin. Used paper towels, pork chop bones and old cans showered down, thunking him on the head.

Lou whimpered and stumbled to his feet. His head was throbbing. Out of half-closed eyes, he saw the cats doing back handsprings across the kitchen linoleum.

"*Ack!* They're *ninja* cats!"

The evil Siamese landed at Lou's feet, slashing the air with their claws.

Lou grabbed the first thing he could find: a can . . . a can! He hauled back to throw it when something curious made him stop.

One of the evil cats had dropped his kung fu stance. His whiskers were twitching. He was eyeing Lou and licking his chops.

Huh? Lou glanced at the can in his paw. A fish was flopping around on the label. He sniffed. Tuna!

Lou flung the can into the corner. The cat dived for it.

"Yes!" Lou yelped, but then his ears sagged.

There was still one Siamese left. And boy, was he mad.

The cat hissed evilly. Just when Lou thought he was going to embarrass himself, he heard Butch's reassuring voice in his collar.

"Okay, kid, just do as I say."

The cat flung a karate chop at Lou's snout.

"Right paw!" Butch barked. Lou shot his right paw up. He blocked the cat's claws!

"Right paw again," Butch hollered. "Duck, duck, back! Up, left, left again! Again!"

Lou couldn't believe it. He was doing kung fu. He was blocking every stab, kick, and karate chop this skinny feline had to offer.

"I changed my mind," Lou yelled as he ducked a lethal tail-whirl. "Call me 'the Claw of Ling Chow'!"

Whomp!

"Ow!" Lou yelped. Out of nowhere, a pawful of claws had snagged him in the nose. Then a hind leg caught him under the chin. He was flying across the room! He landed back in the pile of spilled rubbish.

Lou peeked out from beneath some tinfoil and looked around woozily. He gasped. There were more than two Siamese cats in here!

For the first time, he noticed a third cat creeping along the ceiling, a suction cup on every paw. And there was another, putting a little silver disk into the mouthpiece of the phone. Yet another Siamese was gulping down every goldfish in the Brodys' tank!

Plus, a sixth cat was dangling from a wire in front of the lab door, using a long, silvery instrument to pick the lock!

Nooooo!

"Who's there?!"

Lou gulped. It was Mrs. Brody! She was halfway down the stairs! He saw the lock-picking cat scowl and retract his wire. He zipped toward the ceiling and out of sight. The other cats slunk into the shadows, too.

Lou peeked at the stairwell. Mrs. Brody was pale and trembling. She held a baseball bat. And Professor Brody was armed with . . . a baseball glove.

"I have a mitt," the professor shouted, "and I'm not afraid to use – oh . . ."

Mrs. Brody scowled at her silly husband and flipped the light switch on. She pushed and prodded the professor into the kitchen.

Lou staggered out of the pile of rubbish and looked up at his new owners.

Uh-oh.

"*Lou*," Mrs. Brody scolded.

Before he knew what hit him, Lou had been scooped up and deposited onto the back porch.

Mrs. Brody glanced at the mess in the kitchen. "You're lucky you're so cute," she said to Lou as she slid the glass door closed.

Lou sighed and plopped onto one of the porch steps.

Bzzzzzz.

What was that? Blearily, the puppy looked up and

saw – the ninja cats! They were flying away in tiny toy airplanes! The planes made sinister shadows across the full moon as they buzzed into the night.

"Yeah, you better run, you slimy Siamese cats!" Lou barked.

"Doom Machine!"

It was Sam! He and Peek came bounding into the back yard through the fence plank.

"You're still alive!" Sam panted with joy.

"Yep." Peek peered at Lou. "All four limbs. Sam, you owe me five pig ears. Hickory smoked!"

Butch emerged from some bushes and walked over to join them.

"You all right, kid?" he asked.

At the sight of his boss, Lou leapt to his feet.

"You bet I am! Did you see when I had them going? With a left and a right and—"

"and then you got cocky," Butch barked sternly. "You think this is a game? You think this is fun? This isn't about code names, little boys, or making friends – it's about guarding that lab. *Nothing else.*"

All the happiness drained out of Lou. He hung his head and sniffled.

Butch whirled around to address Sam and Peek. "The cats got in through the chimney. Seal it!"

Without another glance at Lou, Butch stalked away. While Sam and Peek went off to do their chore, Lou skulked into the yard. Boy, had he messed up, big time.

CLANG.

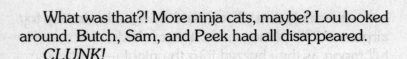

What was that?! More ninja cats, maybe? Lou looked around. Butch, Sam, and Peek had all disappeared.

CLUNK!

The puppy took a deep, trembly breath and followed the sound. He tiptoed around the corner of the house into the alley where the Brodys kept their dustbins.

And one of those dustbins was . . . shaking!

Lou gasped quietly. He inched forward.

Now the can was shimmying. And shuddering. And then it fell over. And out tumbled – a dog!

A dog.

Lou sighed in relief as a silky silver weimaraner scrambled to her feet. She spotted Lou.

"Hi!" she said in a scritchy-scratchy voice. "Can I show you something terrific?"

She motioned for Lou to join her at the mouth of the fallen dustbin. Then she showed him a bunch of bones with some white stuff hanging off them. Lou sniffed at them curiously as the dog prattled on.

"Look at it." She nudged the carcass with her nose. "The Brodys have the best garbage on the block. Go on, take a bite. But mind the dead flies. They're for me."

Lou sniffed again and gave the weimaraner a sidelong look. She nodded encouragingly, so Lou took a nibble.

"Whoa!" he exclaimed. "You mean this is what *they* get to eat? What a gyp!"

"I'm glad I'm not the only one excited by chicken,"

the weimaraner said with a giggle. "I was beginning to think I've been a stray too long."

"Stray?" Lou said with his mouth full of chicken. "Cool. I've never met a stray."

"Actually, I prefer 'domestically challenged'," the weimaraner said, batting her eyelashes.

"Well, Miss Challenged." The puppy became all business. "I'm sorry, but I think you gotta leave. My orders are—"

"Orders?"

"That's right," Lou said, thrusting out his chest. "I'm a *secret agent*."

"An agent!" The weimaraner's blue eyes twinkled. "You're a little small for an agent. Shouldn't you be busy having fun?"

"I don't have time for fun," Lou declared, trying to growl like Butch. "A good agent keeps his mind on his mission and nothing else."

"Oh, I *see*," the dog said dryly. "You're a moron."

"Hey, you're lucky I don't know what that means! Maybe you should get out of my yard!"

"Ohhhh, tough guy."

Then the dog flicked out her paw and began to scratch Lou's ear.

Ooooooooooh. It . . . felt . . . so . . . good. Lou tried to stop his leg from thumping, but he couldn't help it.

As she scratched, the weimaraner reprimanded him.

"Stop with the agent stuff, okay? *You have your*

very own kid to play with. Trust me, don't take it for granted."

Abruptly, she stopped scratching and padded away.

"Whoa!" Lou called, blinking hazily. "Hey, where are you going? Could you do that again?"

The dog shook her head at him.

"Next time the boy talks to you, just tilt your head and perk up your ears. You'll see what I'm talking about. And by the way, the name's Ivy."

With that, she disappeared around the corner.

Chapter Seven

Calico was curled happily in his favourite hiding place – Mr. Mason's medical waste bin. He peeked out through a hole he'd gouged in the aluminum.

Blech – there was Mr. Mason, lying in his hospital bed. The old man was yellow-skinned, wrinkle-pussed and ancient. He was hooked up to about a million tubes and wires. His milky eyes stared into space, and his heart monitor beeped rhythmically next to the bed.

Calico could also see the glowing green eyes of the Tabby, who happened to be hiding in the laundry basket. And there was the wily Manx, crouched under the hospital bed.

Ugh – and here came Sophie.

"Meester Ma-son," sang Sophie's voice from the hallway. "I have someone to see you."

Calico ducked deeper inside the yucky dustbin.

Sophie burst into the room, holding Mr. Tinkles. The Persian was fluffed beyond all recognition. There were bows around each ankle. And on his head was a

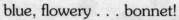

blue, flowery . . . bonnet!

Calico clapped his paws over his mouth to contain his laughter.

Mr. Mason must have found Mr. Tinkles funny, too – as hilarious as a heart attack.

Boooooooop.

The heart monitor went wild. Sophie calmly deposited Mr. Tinkles onto the bed. Then she placed two silver paddles on the old man's chest, sending a jolt of electricity into his heart.

Beep. Beep. Beep.

With Mr. Mason's heart restarted, Sophie returned her attention to Mr. Tinkles.

"You *see* how happy you make him?" she cooed to the cat. "You make his heart go *'boooooop'*! Now I'll leave you two alone."

Sophie bustled out of the room. As soon as she closed the door, Mr. Tinkles slashed at his bonnet. He ripped it to shreds before tossing it to the floor.

"Evil does not wear a *bonnet!*" he raged. He jumped onto Mr. Mason's chest and tried to look fierce. Which was pretty much impossible, since Sophie had also tied a big blue bow between his ears.

"Heh-heh-heh-heh," Calico snickered. Then he watched Mr. Tinkle's squashy face blanch as he felt the bow with his paw.

"Uh . . . sometimes evil wears a ribbon," the Persian covered. "But never a bonnet! *Anyway.* The ninjas failed. And failure is unacceptable. If they ever show their faces again, you know what to do."

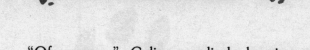

"Of course," Calico replied, leaping onto Mr. Mason's chest to join his boss. "I already told them not to expect a recommendation letter."

"This can't be happening!" Mr. Tinkles screamed. "*I want them killed!*"

"But the ninjas did manage to bug the phone," Calico pointed out. "Maybe we can look at the glass as half full."

"Oh, putting a happy face on things, I see," Mr. Tinkles sneered. "An interesting philosophy."

He shoved his face into Calico's, blasting him with sour fish breath.

"At what point did you forget that we are trying to take over the world?!"

While Calico cringed, Mr. Tinkles flicked his tail carelessly, bonking Mr. Mason on the nose.

"Tomorrow," the Persian said with an evil grin, "you will send the Russian."

Chapter Eight

*L*ou wasn't allowed back into the Brody house until the next morning. He tried to be as good as possible while Mrs. Brody ran around, getting ready to leave for work.

She sipped coffee, typed on her laptop computer, packed Scott's lunch, and swiped dog hair off her suit – all at the same time.

Finally, she slammed the computer shut, popped Scott's lunch into his backpack, and headed for the front door. Lou trotted after her.

"You be a good boy, Lou," she said. "No more mess ups, okay? Speaking of which, maybe you can shed just a tiny bit less."

Lou giggled. Mrs. Brody leaned down close to his face. "How about a kiss?"

Lick, lick, lick. Mmm, Mrs. Brody's makeup tasted good.

Mrs. Brody straightened and yelled up the stairs.

"Good luck with tryouts, Scotty! We'll celebrate

tonight."

"Thanks, Mom!"

"Even if you mess up!" Mrs. Brody cringed when she realized what she had said.

Way to go, Mrs. B. Lou rolled his eyes. Talk about a mess up.

"Uh, not that you will mess up!" Mrs. Brody tried again. "'Cause I know you won't! But if you do, I'll still believe in you. That doesn't mean that you will. It just means that—"

"Mom," Scott yelled wearily. "Leave."

Mrs. Brody sighed and walked out the door.

Scott stomped down the stairs, bouncing his soccer ball on his knee. When he hit the landing, he caught Lou staring at him.

"What?"

Ooooh, Lou seethed. He'll *never* like me.

But suddenly he remembered something Ivy had told him the night before.

Lou tilted his head and perked up his ears. He gazed up at Scott in adoration.

Scott's scowl immediately melted away.

"Well," he said, giving Lou a tiny smile. "I guess you are kinda cute."

Yesssss!

"Scotty?"

Professor Brody, looking frazzled as usual, emerged from the lab and walked into the front hall.

"Last night, your mother and I had, uh, a 'conversation'," the professor said awkwardly. "And I

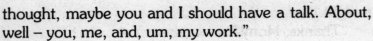

thought, maybe you and I should have a talk. About, well – you, me, and, um, my work."

"Okay."

"I think it's important that you understand that what I'm doing could help a lot of people," Professor Brody began. "But it's also about us. Just think, if this works out, we'll become a complete family. You, me, Mom, and little furry, um, uh . . ."

"Lou."

"Right," the professor said absently. "All of us playing in the park together like it should be. Wouldn't that make all this work worthwhile?"

"I guess. Yeah."

"But talking to your mother did make me think, and, well, I'm going to come to your tryouts this afternoon."

"Nah, you don't have t—"

"No," Professor Brody said firmly. "I'll be there."

Finally, Scott let his face light up with joy.

"Really? Well, okay . . ."

"Now you better get to school." Professor Brody looked pleased with himself as he marched happily back to the lab.

Scott walked out the door with a big grin on his face.

That went well! Lou thought. Now I can have a nice, relaxing mor—

"We got a cat! Bogey in the wire!"

It was Peek, bellowing through Lou's collar.

"You got him, Sam?" Peek asked desperately.

LOU, THE BEAGLE, wants to be a boy's best friend, but Scott would rather hang out with his dad, Professor Brody.

PROFESSOR BRODY works around the clock to find a cure for dog allergies.

MR. TINKLES may look like a friendly feline, but he's secretly planning to take over the world.

THE NINJA CATS AND A RUSSIAN BLUE help Mr. Tinkles put his evil plot into action.

IT'S UP TO LOU and his "agent" friends to save the Brody family from Mr. Tinkles and his crew of cats.

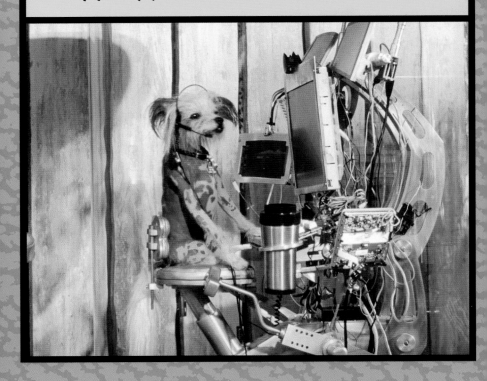

JUST IN TIME, it's Lou to the rescue!

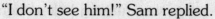

"I don't see him!" Sam replied.

"You *gotta* get a haircut! He's closing fast," Peek yelled. "Right on top of you."

Suddenly the sound of braking tyres screeched through Lou's collar. Come to think of it, Lou could hear the same sound right outside the door . . .

"Oh, no!" Sam bellowed. "It's Mrs. Brody. A bogey staged a car hit. She's bringing the enemy inside."

"Break, break," Peek squealed. "Butch! Code Red!"

Lou was in a panic by the time the front door flew open. Mrs. Brody rushed inside. She was cupping something in her hands.

"Thank goodness I didn't hurt her," she breathed.

"Look, Lou," she said, leaning down. "She's just a poor lost kitty. Don't eat her, okay?"

Mrs. Brody opened her hands to reveal the evil bogey – a tiny Russian blue kitten with sweet round eyes, silky, silvery fur, and the cutest meow Lou had ever encountered. As Lou sniffed the kitten suspiciously, it began purring. Then it nuzzled Lou's neck.

"Awwww," Mrs. Brody cooed. "Look how much she likes you."

Mrs. Brody whipped a phone out of her purse and dialed.

"David, I hit a little snag here," she said into the phone. "You'll have to start showing the house without me."

"*Hack-hack-ack.*"

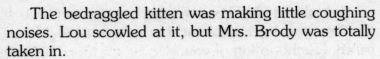
The bedraggled kitten was making little coughing noises. Lou scowled at it, but Mrs. Brody was totally taken in.

"What is it?" she crooned, hanging up the phone. "A hairball? I'll get you some water."

Mrs. Brody click-click-clicked into the kitchen. When she was gone, Lou pointed an accusing paw at the kitten.

"I'm on to you, *kitty*," he said, "and you're in big trouble. *Grrrrrr*."

The kitten's big, sweet eyes suddenly went slitty and venomous. His squeaky little meow morphed into the throaty, Russian-accented growl of a full-grown male feline agent.

"I sink not, baby puppy!" the kitten said. "Eet ees you who ees in trouble. *Hack-ack-ack*."

With a final disgusting retch, the kitten coughed up an enormous hairball. He smirked at Lou and twisted the soggy clump in his claws. Lou saw that it wasn't a hairball at all: It was an aluminum container. Lou craned his head to see what was inside. Oh, no! Dog poop! A big stinking pile of it!

Before Lou could react, the kitten dumped the poop onto the hall rug.

Click. Click. Click.

Mrs. Brody was coming back!

"Lou!"

Mrs. Brody stood over him, furiously eyeing the poop. And faster than you can say "framed," she tossed Lou onto the back porch.

"I do not have time for this!" she yelled. "*Bad* dog!" She slid the glass door shut.

"Is she crazy?" Lou scowled at the door. "That steamer was bigger than me!" Butch's voice rumbled out of Lou's collar.

"What have we got?!" he asked.

"I'm at the front window. It's a Russian blue!" Peek answered.

"And a number two in Sector Three," Sam huffed.

"Of all the rookie mistakes," Butch growled. In an instant, the lab himself had bounded onto the back porch.

"Okay, you're sitting this one out," he barked at Lou, shaking his jowls in disappointment. Butch pushed his collar button.

"Sam, let me know when she leaves."

"I don't see her," Lou heard Sam say. "I think she – oooh, here she comes. Quick, Peek, act like a dog. Uhhh . . . *here*, I'll sniff your butt."

"Ooooh, cold nose, Sam," Peek squealed. "Cold nose!"

Next, Lou heard Mrs. Brody's voice crackle through his collar.

"Get out of it," she said irritably. "Scram!"

A few seconds later, her car started and the dogs were on their own.

Butch sprang into action. He reached for his collar and snapped off his red name tag. When he nosed a tiny button on the tag, a blade popped out. It was a glass cutter. The lab began to cut a hole into the sliding glass door – big enough for a dog to fit through, but small enough to be hidden later by a well-placed potted plant.

While Butch worked on the glass, Lou peeked in at the Russian blue. He could see it in the hallway, gazing at the lab door. Then the cat began hacking and retching. In a few seconds, a huge hairball plopped wetly out of its mouth. Then another one came up. And another.

"Gross!" Lou said, sticking out his tongue. Then he realised he was all alone on the porch. Butch had already slipped inside. Lou knew he was supposed to stay outside, but he couldn't help himself. He wiggled through the hole and crept up behind Butch, who was hiding in the kitchen. Together, they watched the kitten in action.

The Russian began by slapping one of his disgusting hairballs onto the lab door. It stuck like a giant bogey. Then the kitten splatted on another clump, and another. When every hairball was stuck to the door, the evil Russian began connecting them with coloured cables. Finally, he hooked a digital timer to the hairballs and set it for two minutes.

"Huh," Lou blurted out. "What's he doing?"

"Lou!" Butch chastised him.

The Russian whirled around.

"*Ha!* Dogs!" the kitty screamed. Instantly the Russian hacked up another hairball and flung it at Butch and Lou. As it flew through the air, the wet wad of hair transformed into a deathball, with dozens of glinting blades. It landed with a lethal *thwack*, missing Lou's nose by a centimetre.

"*Ha!* Missed!" Lou called. "Oh, nooooo!"

The deathball was coming to life! Its blades started whirling and zinging at the dogs.

"Run!" Butch cried. They took off towards the living room. The deathball followed! Lou glanced over his shoulder to see the ball fling a dozen razor-sharp prongs right at their butts!

"*Aaaaaigh,*" Lou cried as he and Butch dived behind a couch.

Thunk. Thunk. Thunk. Thunk.

The prongs sank deep into Mrs. Brody's Italian upholstery. *Phew,* Lou thought. That was a close one.

A few seconds later, Butch and Lou crept out from behind the couch.

"Oh, doggies?"

Lou whirled around to see the kitten in the living room doorway. He was wearing a knife-thrower's vest! It was all slimy and fuzzy. Clearly, the bottomless Russian had hacked up another lethal trick hairball. The cat began winging one knife after another at Butch and Lou.

"Die, die, die!" he screamed.

The dogs dived back behind the couch. Knives pierced end tables, pillows, flower vases. Feathers and wood chips flew through the air.

"Butch!" It was Sam, panting in the lab's collar. "There's a bomb on the la—"

"Yeah, yeah, we're on it," Butch growled.

He pointed at Lou and whispered, "You're going to distract the Russian."

"*I'm* going to distract him?" Lou squeaked. "Why me?!"

"You said you wanted to help!" Butch shoved Lou out in front of the couch. Then he skulked in the opposite direction, heading for the lab door.

"Hey, you," Lou whispered, "stupid cat . . ."

Thwack, thwack, thwack, thwack, thwack.

"Yip!"

As five knives barely missed Lou's tail, he leapt back behind the couch. Then he watched Butch streak across the living room. Oh, no! The Russian had seen him, too! He began zinging blades at Butch.

Crash, smash, clank! Vases, lamps, and picture frames shattered under the deadly assault.

Butch crouched to duck one knife, then faked a left to avoid another.

Zing!

A blade was heading right for Butch's heart! The old lab sprang into the air, getting a paw-hold on the bookshelf that held the Brodys' TV and stereo.

Creeaaaaak!

Butch was too heavy! The entertainment centre was starting to lean. He lost his balance and tumbled to the floor.

Creeeaaaakk!

Oh, no! Lou thought. It's gonna fall. Butch is a goner!

Creeeaaaa—

It stopped! Lou looked up. The corner of the bookshelf had snagged in some curtains! It hovered just inches from Butch's head as a VCR and a bunch of tapes rained down around him.

"Go, Butch!" Lou yelled.

"I'm tryin'," Butch yelled back, kicking at something wrapped around his hind legs. "Darn Nintendo cords!"

"*Krrrrrggh*, Butch!" It was Peek, yelling through Butch's collar. "You've got one minute!"

"I told you," Butch growled, "we're on it."

Lou ran to the other end of the couch to spy on the Russian. The kitten was eyeing the curtain stretched between the window and the entertainment centre. He snickered. Then he began to retch again.

Hack-ack-ack!

He coughed up another hairball. This one was a boomerang edged by a glinting steel blade. But just as the dastardly Russian was hauling back to fling the blade at the drape, a sound froze the animals in their tracks.

Click-click-click.

Mrs. Brody! She was back! She walked through the hallway and – didn't take one glance through the living room door. Lou heard her in the kitchen, grabbing her forgotten cell phone.

Click-click-click.

Here she came again! Surely her eye would catch the chaos and ruin in the living room. Lou cringed. He could see Mrs. Brody heading for the door. Her head was angling. She was gonna seeeeeeee . . .

Whew. She was just messing with her earring.

Slam!

She was gone.

The kitten instantly unfroze.

"Hi-ya!" he screamed. He threw the boomerang. The blade neatly caught the curtain, but it only cut into part of it. The curtain still held the bookshelf up by a thread.

The lethal blade whizzed back into the kitten's waiting paw. He was going to throw it again. Lou had to do something. He charged out from behind the couch and galloped toward his boss.

"Hang on, Butch!" he yelled.

"Hey, puppy," the Russian called. And then he uttered those fatal words, the words that no foxhound can possibly resist.

"Fetch!"

"No! Wait!" Butch bellowed.

But Lou was helpless. He saw the boomerang fly into the air and leaped into its path. With his jaws opened wide, he lunged to catch it.

The boomerang caught him in the chest. Luckily, it was the dull side of the blade. Still, Lou was caught on the thing like a burr in dog fur. He whizzed around the living room.

"*AAAAAIIIGGGH – ooof!*"

Lou crashed into the kitten. Together they slid into the hallway and landed just outside the lab door.

As Lou and the kitten rolled across the floor in paw-to-paw combat, Lou heard a crash in the living room.

The bookcase! Butch! *Nooooooo!*

It only took that instant of distraction for the Russian to get the upper paw. He gripped Lou's neck in his claws, choking him.

"*Aaaaiggh, arrrrgh,*" Lou grunted, gasping for breath. Then he saw something out of the corner of his eye, something that made his heart soar, even as he fought for his life.

It was Butch! He'd escaped! He was standing in front of the lab door. And the timer – it said three seconds!

"Hurry! The bomb!" Sam and Peek yelled through Butch's collar.

"The book says to cut the red wire," Peek instructed.

"We're dogs," Butch yelled. "We're colour-blind!"

"Oh, yeah!" Peek remembered. "The dark grey one!"

Butch bit through the wire just as the timer hit 0:00. Lou was so happy, he found a surge of strength.

"*Grrrowr!*" he shouted, tossing the kitten off him. The Russian flew through the air. But somehow he executed an expert triple flip and landed on his feet in front of Butch.

"You think you haf von?" he demanded. "*Hack-ack-ack!*"

He retched yet another small device into his paw. It had a big button on it.

"Remote detonator!" the kitten announced. "Ha!"

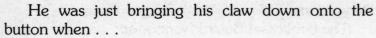
He was just bringing his claw down onto the button when . . .

Slam!

The lab door flew open! The Russian was swept against the wall behind the door with a crunch. Lou saw Butch skitter out of the hallway just as Professor Brody stormed out of the lab. His head was covered with electrodes and wires, and his eyes were practically spinning with excitement.

"Lou!" he called. "Here, boy! Come!"

The professor looked around wildly before he noticed Lou, sprawled at his feet.

"Oh!" Professor Brody exclaimed. He whipped out another shot and injected himself with a glowing orange liquid.

"Okay," the professor murmured, scooping up Lou and taking a deep sniff. Lou trembled, wondering if the evil Russian was gonna pull a fast one. But the kitten was nowhere to be seen.

Lou glanced back at the professor.

"Yip!"

The man's skinny nose was swelling. And swelling. And swelling! It was the size of an orange!

The professor glanced at a mirror on the wall and grinned.

"Bulbous, but no sneezing!" he announced. "This is good! No, this is better than good. A *breakthrough*!"

Suddenly Professor Brody gave Lou a loud kiss and plopped him back onto the floor.

"Good boy," he crowed, heading back into the lab.

"Now I just need to find that one sequence. . . ."

Slam!

The lab door closed, revealing the crushed Russian blue. He was out cold.

Butch crept back into the hall and nosed the limp kitten. Then he galloped to the front door to let in Sam and Peek.

"Take care of the kitty and clean this place up," he ordered. "I'll work out a cover story for Mom."

Butch turned to Lou.

"And kid . . ."

Lou cringed. He knew he'd messed up, following Butch into the house like that. He waited for his boss to bawl him out.

"Good thinking with the boomerang," Butch said with a rough smile. "Now you're acting like an agent."

Without waiting for a response, the lab bounded out the door.

"Ha!" Lou was pleased with the praise.

"Whoa," Peek said, "was that a *compliment*?"

"Must be battle fatigue," Sam said. "I saw a lot of that in W-W-Seven. Tragic . . ."

"Shut up," Peek said, swatting Sam's shaggy head. He grinned at Lou. "The pup did good."

Chapter Nine

Hours later, Mrs. Brody arrived home. Lou sat in the hallway waiting for her. He panted in greeting, smiling up at her as cutely as he possibly could. But she barely looked at him. Instead she peered down the hallway and pulled a little rubber mouse out of her suit pocket.

"Here, kitty," she called. "Got a treat for you."

The "kitty," of course, did not come. Mrs. Brody began clicking around the house, searching for him. When she headed into the living room, Lou held his breath, but she didn't notice a thing! Except a window left open and the curtain billowing in the breeze.

"Oh, no!" Mrs. Brody said. "The kitty must have gotten out and run away." She shook her head. "First the goldfish and now this . . ."

Click-click-click.

Mrs. Brody headed through the kitchen with Lou trotting right behind her. They found Scott in the back yard, scowling, dribbling his soccer ball across the grass. Boy, was he mad.

"Scotty?" Mrs. Brody called. "You haven't seen a little . . . oh."

She eyed the soccer ball and Scott's angry frown.

"Tryouts," she remembered. "I guess it didn't go so well, huh? I'm sorry . . ."

"I sucked." Scott spit the words out. "Worse than sucked."

"Oh, I'm sure you're exaggerating," Mrs. Brody replied, walking onto the grass. "What did the coach say?"

"He told me tryouts for the girls' team are on Monday."

"What? That sexist," Mrs. Brody said. "Well . . . what about your dad?"

Whack!

Scott kicked the ball so hard, it disappeared into a bush.

"He wasn't there, was he?" Mrs. Brody clenched her teeth. "Okay . . ."

Click-click-click-click-click.

Uh-oh, Lou thought. I've gotta see this. He tailed Mrs. Brody into the house. She banged on the lab door with her fist. A moment later, Professor Brody appeared. Electrodes and wires still stuck out all over his head, making him look like a robotic hedgehog.

"Hey, honey," the professor said hurriedly. "I'm in the middle of a—"

"Soccer?" Mrs. Brody demanded.

"No, thanks," her husband replied. "I – oh, no!

I forgot!"

He grabbed Mrs. Brody's hands. "But it's only because I had a breakth—"

"I know your work is important to you," she sputtered. "But in case you forgot, *he's your son!*"

"You're right," the professor said. "I'm sorry, I . . ."

Lou hung his head as the professor tried to explain. How come humans could be so dumb? he wondered. Lou ambled out to the back yard, where he found Scott miserably slumped on the porch steps.

Lou scanned the yard. Ah-ha! Spotting a bruised-looking bush, he trotted over to the shrub and burrowed beneath it. He emerged pushing Scott's soccer ball in front of him. He batted it towards the boy.

When the ball hit Scott's foot, he looked over at Lou. A smile began at the corners of his mouth.

"Good boy," he whispered, patting Lou on the head.

Suddenly a warm feeling washed over Lou. It was better than chicken, even better than ear-scratching. This kid *liked* him! It was about time. Lou never knew having a boy of his own would feel so cool.

Lou barked and ran out into the yard.

"Okay, okay," Scott laughed. He got to his feet and kicked the ball over to Lou. Lou nudged the ball back to Scott. Before long, boy and dog were hard at play.

It was the best hour of Lou's life.

But eventually Mrs. Brody called Scott in for

dinner. Lou was following his boy inside when a familiar bark stopped him in his tracks.

"Lou!" It was Butch, standing at the open fence plank. "Into the house!"

Lou gave Scott a last longing look. Then he obeyed orders and trotted over to his kennel. Sam and Peek were already inside, glued to the video monitor.

Russian blue kitten was on the screen! He was locked in a dank-looking, bare room. All his limbs, even his tail, were strapped to a chair. And a bright lamp was aimed at his squinty eyes.

Suddenly a meaty dog paw slapped the kitten across the face. The Russian barely flinched. In fact, he grinned through a mouthful of blood and spit.

"I vill tell you nothing," the Russian said. "Do you know how many painful operations I had to go through to look this way? I may look cute and cuddly, but inside . . . granite."

"*Cute?*" said a dog offscreen. He must have been one of the interrogators. "Who said you looked cute?"

In an instant, the Russian's smarmy scowl was replaced by a wide-eyed look of sweet innocence.

"*Meow,*" he cooed.

"Awwwww," said another offscreen voice.

"*Paul!*" barked the first dog. "And you call yourself a professional!"

Suddenly the collie's long nose filled the screen.

"I don't think we're going to get anything else out of him, Butch," he said. "But look over here."

The camera swerved to take in a table filled with

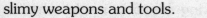
slimy weapons and tools.

"We pumped the Russian's stomach and found a few things," the collie explained. "Including this."

In his paws, he held a moist bit of stationery with scrawled handwriting on it. It was clearly the penmanship of a madcat.

"'This is the address where you are to enact my fiendish plan,'" Butch read. "'P.S. Eat this note after you read it so no one will find it.'"

"But look here," the collie said.

The camera zoomed in on a corner of the stationery. It was stamped with a spiky green pine tree.

"A Christmas tree," the collie said. "Research is trying to place it, but they haven't turned up anything. Ring any bells?"

Butch shook his head.

"Well, global tensions are heating up like a minivan on a summer day," the collie said. "So just keep guarding that lab. The world has placed its destiny in your paws."

Click.

The screen went blank.

The dogs returned to the yard.

"You heard her, boys – focus on the mission," Butch said. "Peek, I want full-spread scans every twenty minutes. Sam, trim your fringe. Now move out."

As Sam and Peek trotted away, Butch turned to Lou.

"And kid?" he said. "Keep up the good work. I know I don't need to remind you to stay away from the boy. Just keep your eye on the ball."

"Yes, sir!" Lou barked happily.

As Butch left, Lou marched towards the house. He wore a warrior's scowl.

"Keep my eye on the ball," he muttered. "Righty-oh, nooooo problem. Just gotta keep my eye on the—"

"Hey, Lou!"

It was Scott. He was standing on the back porch with a pocket full of doggy biscuits and . . . a ball.

Before he knew it, Lou was leaping through the air, bopping the soccer ball with his forehead. He kicked the ball through invisible goals. He blocked Scott's shots with his nose.

"Good dog!" Scott said.

"*Arf, arf!*" Lou barked. He ran around his boy – his very own boy. Lou was elated. He was a puppy fulfilled. He was a puppy . . . with no short-term memory.

Early the next morning, Scott and Lou were at it again. Lou was doing his famous fakeout, stealing the ball away from Scott.

"Is that your ball?" Scott laughed. "Oh, you think so?"

"*Growr,*" Lou answered.

"*Growr-growr,*" Scott replied. Then he pointed to the back fence. "A cat!"

"*Arp!*" Lou yelled, whirling around to face the intruder. Of course, that was Scott's big fakeout. By

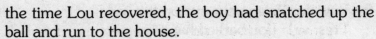

the time Lou recovered, the boy had snatched up the ball and run to the house.

"*Woof, woof, woof.*" Lou chased Scott into the kitchen. He pounced onto Scott playfully, a little *too* playfully. The ball sprang out of the boy's hands.

"Uh-oh!" Scott cried.

"*Yip,*" Lou yelped.

Bounce-bounce-bounce-b-b-b-b-bounce . . .

Talk about not keeping his *eye* on the ball! Lou gulped as he watched the soccer ball shoot through the lab door, which for some reason had been left open. And now the ball careered down the lab steps.

Scott raced down the stairs with Lou at his heels.

At the last step, Lou looked around wildly. He saw the professor's lab table, which was loaded with graphs and notes. And there was a humming computer. Lou also spotted a jar of bubbling orange liquid – the professor's latest formula.

But where was the ball?

Scott gasped and pointed.

There it was, teetering on the edge of a shelf right above the lab table. It seemed to tremble for a moment. Then it paused.

It's gonna stick, Lou thought. He breathed a sigh of relief.

That was when the ball fell.

It was heading straight for the jar of orange liquid!

Before Lou could think twice about it, he leaped into the air.

"Lou, no!" Scott cried. But Lou had to remember

his mission: Protect the lab at all costs!

He made a direct hit! He head-butted the ball, sending it over the lab table.

The ball missed the beaker. Yessss! Lou thought.

But then it crashed straight into a rack against the wall – a rack filled with bottles, jars, beakers, pots, and bowls of chemicals.

Noooooo!

With an earsplitting shatter, the glass containers hit the floor. Chemicals flew everywhere. Rainbow-coloured liquids formed a river on the floor.

"My work!"

Professor Brody stood on the bottom step, gaping at the ruins of his lab. Scott gasped and spun around to face his father.

"I'm sooooo sorry, Dad," he began to apologise. "It was an accident. The door was open, and—"

"I think," the professor said in a trembling voice, "you should go to school."

Scott nodded sadly and squeezed past the professor. He ran up the stairs and disappeared.

Lou cowered with his tail between his legs. What had he done? He'd ruined everything, that's what! The world had placed its destiny in his paws, and he'd totally blown it!

"Butch is gonna kill me," Lou whispered, his lower lip trembling.

The professor's lip was doing a shimmy of its own as he picked through the spilled chemicals. Lou watched him kick at a computer sensor that had fallen into the puddle.

Whiirrrr. Bleep. Bleeeeeeep.

"Huh?" the professor said. He peered at his computer screen. It was going wild. "What the heck?"

Suddenly the professor gasped. He swept all the broken clutter off his lab table and stormed over to Lou. He scooped the puppy up and planted him on the table. Next the professor filled a hypodermic needle with the swirling rainbow liquid and plunged the shot into his arm.

Then, his eyes bulging with excitement, Professor Brody buried his nose in Lou's fur. He breathed deeply and waited.

Nothing happened.

He took another deep whiff and waited some more.

Nothing happened. No sneezes. No sniffles. No green spots. No nothin'.

"Yeesssss!" the professor hollered. He grabbed Lou and galloped upstairs.

"I did it! We did it! Yes. Yes. Yesssssss!"

A few minutes later, Professor Brody was on the phone. Lou was still cradled in his arms, so he could hear every word.

"Yes!" Professor Brody said. "I told you (*click*) it was possible – an actual (*click*) cure for dog allergies!"

"Charlie," said the man in the phone, "this is (*click*) wonderful! I want to get this into production ASAP. When can (*click*) you send it?!"

Hmmm, Lou wondered. What's that clicking?

"If I can verify everything tonight," the professor crowed, "it'll be (*click*) ready in the morning!"

He hung up, plopped Lou onto the floor, and dashed down to the lab. Lou giggled with joy and trotted to the kitchen for some celebratory puppy chow.

And that curious clicking? Lou forgot about that faster than you can say "ninja Siamese cat."

Chapter Ten

"If I can verify everything tonight" – the professor's voice clearly carried into Mr. Mason's bedroom – "it'll be ready in the morning!"

"Blast!" Mr. Tinkles screeched from his perch atop Mr. Mason's chest. He shot a fluffy paw out and swatted a radio receiver from the old man's nightstand. The radio crashed to the floor and shattered. Professor Brody's voice died with a squawk.

So much for the ninja cats' phone bug, Calico thought with a sigh. He rolled his eyes at the Manx, who was sitting on the floor next to him. Calico shoved the crushed radio underneath the bed and looked up at his boss. The Persian was stomping on Mr. Mason's ribs in rage.

"This is unacceptable!" he screeched. "If we do not act immediately, that work will be out of my reach forever! Do you know what that means?"

"Who, me?" Calico blurted. "Uh . . ."

"Were you not paying attention?" Mr. Tinkles demanded.

"Not really," Calico said, trying to look innocent. "Are you angry?"

"*Yes, I am angry,* you little bug of an imbecile wrapped in incompetence whose very visage makes the contents of my stomach lose their grasp!" Mr. Tinkles screamed. "I'll take a knitting needle so long and—"

"Meeester Teeenkles!"

It was Sophie, coming to torment the Persian once again. Calico and the Manx darted under the bed with a snicker. They watched Sophie plump into the room. She held out a tiny maid's outfit just like hers – frilly white apron and all.

"Look what I brought for you, Meeester Teeenkles," Sophie exclaimed. "Now you can look like me!"

There was a sinister pause. And then the great Persian . . . spoke!

"No, I think not, Sophie," he said dryly. "Those days are through."

Whoa! Calico thought. That's my cue! He slunk out from beneath the bed, hissing at Sophie. The Manx was right behind him, cackling.

The maid froze. Her eyes glazed over. Her chins trembled.

"What's the matter?" Mr. Tinkles asked. "Cat got your tongue?"

"*Urgle,*" Sophie gasped. Then she fell to the floor in a dead faint.

Mr. Tinkles leapt to the floor and cried, "Lock her

in the closet. We must remain on schedule. *Our day has come!*"

An hour later, Mr. Mason's chauffeur drove the old man to work in his shiny black limo.

Well, that would be a slight bending of the truth.

In actuality, Calico was behind the wheel of the limo. He was standing on the lap of a mannequin that looked remarkably like a chauffeur. He steered the long black car, while below him, the Manx jumped on the accelerator and the Havana brown handled the brake.

Mr. Mason sat in the back seat. The old guy was still catatonic, his eyes blank and staring. He wore an overcoat with a lump inside it. A lump that would be, of course, Mr. Tinkles. A woollen scarf hid Mr. Mason's mouth.

"There it is! The old man's factory," Calico shouted, whipping the steering wheel to the right. "All right. . . . Slower . . . slower . . . *brake!*"

The limo lurched to a halt at the gate. Calico peeked out the side window and saw a guard booth with a snow-dusted Christmas tree on it.

Mr. Tinkles lowered the back window three inches – just enough for the guard to see Mr. Mason's cloudy blue eyes. The guard jumped to his feet and stared.

"Mr. Mason," he stuttered. "What a surprise, sir."

"Good morning, human guard." Calico heard Mr. Tinkles's voice. "Let us in."

"Of course, sir."

It was all Calico could do not to laugh as the guard raised the gate.

"Gas!" Calico hissed. The Manx hopped on the accelerator and they shot down the driveway.

"Next stop, Mason Tree Flocking, Incorporated," Calico cackled.

When they arrived at the factory, Calico switched from driving the limo to chauffeuring Mr. Mason's electric wheelchair. The cats propped Mr. Mason in the chair with Mr. Tinkles on his lap. Then Calico hid in the chair's battery compartment. The rest of the cats walked casually behind the chair.

Together they rolled into Mr. Mason's factory. Calico peeked through some slits in the battery compartment. He could see a conveyer belt whizzing green trees into a flocking device, a machine that covered the trees in artificial snow. Another assembly line sprayed snow on plastic snowmen.

Calico buzzed the chair across the factory floor.

"Mr. Mason," gasped one employee, eyeing the bundled-up old man. "Ahem, hello, sir."

"Hello," Mr. Tinkles answered. "Out of my way."

"How are you feeling sir?" piped up another worker.

"Out of my way," Mr. Tinkles commanded.

Everybody was so stunned to see their ancient boss out and about that nobody noticed the Persian's lips moving.

Calico buzzed the chair into an elevator at the end of the room. The Manx sprang up and hit a button.

The elevator carried them to the second floor and opened onto a small reception area that fronted Mr. Mason's window-lined office. In his heyday, Calico thought, the old man must have sat behind the glass and gazed down upon his workers. Now the powerful Mr. Tinkles would do the same.

But first they had to get past the receptionist sitting at a desk next to the office door. The woman glanced up from her computer and gasped.

"Mr. Mason?"

"Get the door," Mr. Tinkles ordered.

The receptionist leaped to her feet and obeyed. Calico buzzed the wheelchair inside and spun around so that Mr. Mason faced the woman.

"Can I get you anything, sir?" she asked nervously.

"Sushi and a quart of cream," Mr. Tinkles demanded. "Close the door."

As soon as the woman was gone, Mr. Tinkles pointed at the office window. Calico buzzed them over. The factory workers looked up to see Mr. Mason's expressionless eyes staring down at them.

Then Mr. Tinkles leaped over to the desk. He found an intercom and pressed its button. In an instant, Mr. Tinkles's voice was echoing through the factory.

"Attention, human workers," he said. "This is your employer, Mr. Mason. Effective immediately, you are all *fired.*"

Calico heard a gasp from the factory floor. He giggled.

"Go home now," Mr. Tinkles continued. "Do not

ask why. You have no one to blame but yourselves. Unless, of course, you have a dog – then you can blame him. In fact, kick him when you get home. That is all."

As cries of anguish and murmurs of disbelief floated up from the factory floor, Mr. Tinkles pressed the intercom button once more.

"Long live cats!" he added.

Mr. Tinkles took his paw off the intercom and faced his feline crew.

"Now . . ." he said with a squashy smirk. "Brody's lab!"

Chapter Eleven

A dog's work is never done.

That afternoon, as the professor laboured on his new vaccine, Lou crept along the alley next to the Brodys' house. He touched his collar button.

"Am I close?" he whispered.

Peek's voice crackled quietly out of his collar.

"Other side of the porch," he said. "The shrubs."

Lou crept around the corner and passed the porch, tiptoeing through the grass and sniffing the ground.

"You're almost on him," Sam whispered in Lou's collar. "Three ticks east and he's flanked . . ."

Lou turned to a particular bush. It shivered ever so slightly.

"*Grrrrr-arf!*" Lou yelped, diving into the shrub. A second later, Scott tumbled out, laughing. Lou pounced on the boy's chest, barking and panting happily.

"How do you always find me?" Scott laughed. "Go on, you can tell me."

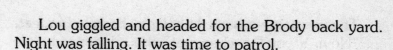

Lou giggled and headed for the Brody back yard. Night was falling. It was time to patrol.

Lou was sitting on the back porch, scanning the darkened yard for bogeys, when he heard a skittering behind him.

"Hey, Lou," said a scritchy-scratchy voice.

The puppy spun around.

"Ivy! Where've you been?!"

"Around," the weimaraner answered as she sat down next to Lou.

"I've been having the most incredible week. I got to beat up a kitten, I'm on wet food, and Scott says I'm his best friend!"

"Terrific!" Ivy said.

"But don't tell anyone," Lou whispered. "Butch wouldn't like it if he found out. He gets mad about that stuff."

"Yeah, I know," Ivy sighed. "But he's not mad. Sometimes mad is just a way of hiding how sad you are."

"What? Why would Butch be sad?"

Ivy paused and said quietly, "It's not my place to say. Let's just say a person really hurt him once."

"But why would someone want to hurt Butch?" Lou wondered.

"People don't always know they're hurting our feelings," Ivy tried to explain.

"Huh?"

"You'll figure it out," she said kindly. "Just part of being a dog."

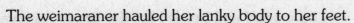
The weimaraner hauled her lanky body to her feet.

"Now, if you'll excuse me," she announced, "it's all-you-can-eat ribs night at the dumpster behind Tony Roma's."

Ivy slunk off the porch and into the night. Lou shook his head and gazed at the bright, full moon, thinking about what Ivy had said.

"Whatcha lookin' at, kid?"

"*Arf!*" Lou yelped, spinning around. He found himself nose to nose with Butch.

"Oh!" he gasped. "Sorry. What's up?"

"Well," Butch said carefully, "Professor's done. I filed my report and, well . . . They're impressed with you, kid. They wanted me to give you this."

Butch held out a red dog tag with tiny buttons on its edges. It was just like the glass cutter Butch had used during the raid of the Russian blue!

"But," Lou stuttered, "This is for an ag—"

"Seems once this job's over, you've got a spot at the academy. You pulled it off, kid. Good work."

"You're kidding! I'd get to be a real agent? Like you?"

"Well," Butch said, allowing himself to grin, "you can *try*."

"We can be *partners*." Lou hopped in place and did a somersault or two.

"Whoa, whoa," Butch rumbled, holding up a paw. "Don't wet the paper just yet. But if you make the cut, just think of the places you'll see. Maybe Burma. Or Denmark. Or Pasadena."

Lou halted in midhop.

"Oh, wait. So, I wouldn't stay here?"

"You go where they need you," Butch said.

Lou plunked down on the porch. Huh. That meant he'd have to leave Scott behind. Lou's floppy ears sagged at the thought.

"Butch . . ." he began.

"Break, break!"

It was Peek's voice crackling urgently out of Butch's collar.

"Bogey in the wire," Peek yelled.

"Where?" Butch demanded.

"Sector 47-B," Peek said.

"I've got a visual." That was Sam. "It's a calico. Should I take him?"

"Negative," Butch said. "Me and the kid got this."

Then Butch winked at Lou. Whoa! Butch was being so . . . nice! Lou grinned and ran after his boss.

The dogs raced around the house and out onto the pavement.

"There he is!" Lou called, pointing at a calico cat. The feline was strutting down the pavement with a big black rectangle clenched in its teeth.

Butch pounced on the cat, growling and barking.

"Okay! Okay! Ow!" Calico cried, spitting out the black thing. It was a videotape. Lou grabbed the tape as Butch continued to rough the cat up.

"Yeah, yeah. You got me! *Oww!*" meowed Calico. "Stop it!"

Butch looked at the tape in Lou's mouth. Then he grabbed the calico.

"Come on," he said. He touched his collar button. "Sam, Peek – into the house."

A few minutes later, the dogs – and their hostage cat – settled into the Brodys' living room. Peek pushed the videotape into the VCR and hit PLAY with his nose. The television sputtered a bit. Then the hideous, squashy face of a white Persian cat filled the screen.

"Hello," the Persian sneered, "my puny-minded dog-faced oppon— what?"

The cat looked to his left and scowled as someone meowed offscreen.

"Yes, it's on!" he said.

There was more muted meowing.

"Because I can see the red light blinking," the cat yelled. "Start over!"

The evil cat composed himself and began again.

"Hello, my puny-minded dog-faced opponents. I'm sure you have wondered to yourselves about the identity of who it is that will defeat you. Who it is that possesses the intellect to win in this chess game of wits and might. Well, look closely. It is I."

Suddenly the tape cut to a grainy, black-and-white film. Lou squinted as he watched a white four-wheel-drive pull into an empty car park.

Hey, he thought, that looks just like the Brodys' car.

When the camera zoomed in, Lou gasped. Professor Brody was leaning out of the car's window, talking to a man in a guard booth.

"We must be early!" Professor Brody laughed, motioning to the empty car park. "Guess that makes us first in line for hot dogs and ice cream. So how much do I owe you?"

The car park guard stood there. He didn't speak. Or move.

"I'm sorry," Professor Brody said, laughing again. "I didn't catch that."

The guard remained silent. But this time, he *did* move. His arm jerked up like a spring.

"It's a robot!" Lou yelled, leaping to his feet.

The "guard" tossed a black canister into the car. The four-wheel-drive's windows filled with smoke! And in a few seconds, all three Brodys had passed out.

Next, the tape showed the family blindfolded and tied up. They sat in a dim room – it looked like some kind of office. Lou gasped again.

"*Heh-heh-heh-heh,*" Calico snickered, until Sam gave him a whack on the head.

The tape cut back to the evil Persian.

"You are to bring the formula and all notes regarding Professor Brody's research to the Ninth Street Bridge at dawn," he ordered. "If you refuse, they will be put to sleep."

"No!" Lou cried, turning to Butch. His boss gritted his teeth and growled.

"And if you have any plans," the Persian continued, "to threaten the life of my messenger, Calico . . ."

Calico slapped Butch on the back and cackled,

"See you later, losers!"

". . . do with him what you will," the Persian finished.

"*Heh-heh-heh,*" Sam said dryly, stepping in Calico's path.

Lou watched the cat's eyes widen with fear as the Persian screeched, "I've had enough of your incompetence, Calico! Good-bye, you foolish imbec—"

The Persian stopped and glanced offscreen.

"Oh, darn, wait," he said. "If I betray him now, he might tell them how I plan to defeat them. Cut. Edit that out."

The Persian resumed his speech.

"So, as for my messenger and *dear, dear friend,* Calico, I expect him to be let go so he may return unharmed. And do not forget your precious humans. You have until dawn to comply. *Ahhhhh-haaaa-haaa-haa-ha!*"

The Persian's evil cackle filled the living room as the dogs stared at the television in shock. Meanwhile, Calico gave Sam a kick and stalked out of the house.

"Butch," Lou quavered, "what do we do? We're gonna save them, right? Right?!"

"This is way over our heads," Butch said, shaking his jowls. "Come with me."

The old lab ejected the videotape and gripped it in his teeth. Leaving Peek and Sam to guard the house, Butch and Lou walked out to the kennel. Butch hit the nail to reveal the videophone and controls.

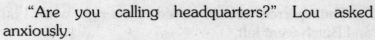

"Are you calling headquarters?" Lou asked anxiously.

"No, kid," Butch rumbled. "We're going there."

With that, the lab hit the Big Button.

Suddenly two chairs erupted from the floor just beneath them. With a yelp, Lou tumbled backwards and plopped into one of them.

A seat belt slithered around his belly, and a plastic hood slammed over his chair. Out of the corner of his eye, Lou saw Butch's chair do the same thing. They were being strapped into their own small rockets!

"Coooool," Lou started to say.

But then the floor vanished and Lou felt himself drop like a shot.

"*AAAAAAAAAAAAAHHHHHHH!*" he screamed.

He and Butch began hurtling through a tunnel. Their speed was so high, Lou could feel his lips stretching back to his ears! There was nothing Lou could do but . . . scream some more.

"*AAAAAAAAAAHHHHHHHHH!*"

Suddenly another rocket pulled up beside Lou's. He turned to peer at it with bulging eyes.

"Squirrels!" he gasped.

That's right. Two squirrels wearing helmets and radio collars were speeding through the tunnel, too. One of the rodents turned to Lou and waved his tiny paw.

"Out of the way, dogs!" he yelled. "Goldfish are trying to take over the world!"

Zoooooom!

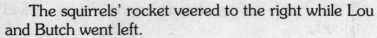

The squirrels' rocket veered to the right while Lou and Butch went left.

Bonk!

They'd arrived. Lou looked around shakily. He and Butch had landed in some sort of holding tank. The plastic shield rotated back and, with trembling legs, the puppy climbed out of his rocket. Butch nodded at him and led him to a door at the end of the room.

Butch placed his paw on a sensor just like the one in the Brodys' fence. It glowed green and the door *whooshed* open. Lou stepped through the door and gazed around, blinking in disbelief. Butch patted him on the back.

"This is it, kid," the old lab said. "Welcome to HQ."

Chapter Twelve

Butch began walking down a long, white hallway lined with windows. Lou stumbled after him.

"I never knew dogs could be so . . . organised," Lou gasped as a lhasa apso trotted by with a stack of papers in her teeth. He also spotted a Scottish terrier rolling a cart of meat-scented danishes into a conference room.

To Lou's right was a huge gymnasium. Lou peered through the windows and admired the dogs inside. Twin dobermans were hefting dumbbells while a basset hound worked the rowing machine. Nearby, a crew of greyhounds ran on treadmills behind a stuffed rabbit.

In the middle of the gym, a pack of huskies in matching grey tank tops kicked their hind legs at punching bags.

"*Heee-yah!*" the dogs barked in unison.

And over in the corner, an airedale barked at a vacuum cleaner while a thick-necked pit bull trainer

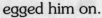

egged him on.

"Cooooool!" Lou breathed.

Next, he peeked into the room on his left. This one was a laboratory. A dachshund in a lab coat stared at a fire hydrant on a table. When she pushed a button at the base of the hydrant, the top flipped open. Then a bazooka popped out and shot at a cat-shaped target on the wall.

The dachshund smiled and made a note on her clipboard.

Lou walked on and saw a scratching post blow up a robotic cat, a dog speaking into a toilet lid videophone, and a gallery of famous dogs in history. And doggy snack vending machines everywhere!

"Kid," Butch muttered. "Stop drooling. You're embarrassing me. Now let's go show this tape to the general."

In minutes, Lou found himself in the hub of headquarters – the control room. All around him, dogs barked into headsets and videophones. Others monitored maps dotted with cat-shaped thumbtacks. Still others typed furiously into computers.

A squat corgi led Butch and Lou to the slobbery-mouthed mastiff, General Charles. Quickly, Butch briefed the mastiff on the situation.

"My God," the general roared wetly. He picked up a red phone.

"Assemble the delegates!" he ordered.

"Whoa," Lou muttered, wiping a gob of spit off his

snout. "Say it, don't spray it!"

"Kiiiid," Butch growled softly.

"All right!" the mastiff yelled, hanging up the red phone. "We've successfully cleared out the Westminster Dog Show semi-finals. Luckily, there was a rocket-launching chute in a 'dustbin' nearby. The delegates will be here any minute. On to the World Dog Council assembly room!"

Wiping a fresh coating of spit off their faces, Butch and Lou followed the mastiff out of the control room. They walked through a series of downward-sloping hallways, turning right, then left, then right again, until Lou was thoroughly lost.

Finally, the dogs emerged in a grand room. On the wall was a huge, elegant mural.

"Humans playing poker," Lou noted. "Niiiice."

The rest of the circular room was filled with row upon row of chairs.

The mastiff led Lou and Butch to the stage at the front of the room as dogs of all nationalities began to pour in.

In a few minutes, every dog was seated and briefed on this latest development in the Brody Brouhaha. Then Lou watched in fascination – and alarm – as the dogs began to debate.

"We cannot tolerate terrorism," announced a wrinkly Chinese shar-pei. "Sadly, the family must be sacrificed."

Lou gasped. A German shepherd spoke up.

"There are lives at stake!" he argued. "We cannot

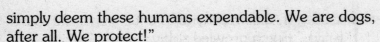

simply deem these humans expendable. We are dogs, after all. We protect!"

"But at what cost?" piped up a French poodle. "It is for ze greater good zat ze Brodys give their lives to save ze rest of humanity from zis rogue cat."

"Our prime minister," shouted an English cocker spaniel, "wishes to address the assembly direct – *Good God!* Um . . . never mind."

Lou glanced at the prime minister and blushed. The cocker spaniel was licking himself where no dog ought to lick himself. Not in public, anyway!

Next a bloodhound spoke up. An American! Lou thought. Surely he'll speak up for my family!

But the bloodhound was only interested in bravado.

"If they had listened to me," he said, leaning back in his chair, "this kitty problem would have been solved a long time ago."

Then he whistled and made a sound like an exploding bomb. The other American dogs tittered.

With that, dozens of dogs leaped to their feet and began debating. It was chaos!

Finally, a majestic Great Dane loped up to the stage. She pounded on a lectern with her paw.

"Delegates," she barked. "Order, please. Order!"

Everyone, of course, ignored her. They went on barking and growling. The Great Dane rolled her eyes and pulled an electric can opener out from beneath her lectern.

Whiiirrrrrrr.

Instantly, the room fell silent. At the wonderful sound of the can opener, every dog stopped talking and started drooling. They stared at the Great Dane.

"Sit!" she ordered.

They sat.

"Now," the enormous dog said. "We have a decision to make: family or formula?"

Five hours later the council was still debating what to do. Butch put a paw on Lou's shoulder.

"We've done all we can do here," he said. "They won't be voting for a while yet. Let's head home."

Nodding wearily, Lou followed Butch back to their rockets. Soon, Lou was screaming his way through another terrifying rocket ride.

Before he knew it, he and Butch had landed back in his kennel.

And things didn't look good.

Peek, Sam, and Ivy were huddled around the video monitor watching the Canine News Network. The pointy-eared anchorman was addressing the camera.

"Wolf Blitzer, CNN. Just minutes ago, the World Dog Council announced the fate of the Brody family. In a dramatic late-night session, the decision was made to keep the Brody formula out of hostile paws at all costs."

"What?" Lou squeaked. "They're not going to save my family?"

"Prominent feline delegates have denounced this terrorist act," Wolf Blitzer continued. The broadcast cut to a striped cat in military garb. He read a statement into a bundle of microphones.

"This cat does *not* represent the peaceful felines of the world," the cat said. "We denounce his actions, no matter how fiendishly clever they may be."

Lou's mouth fell open.

"Oh, no," Ivy said. She put a comforting paw on Lou's head, but he shook it off. He stepped out into the yard.

"Hold on a second, kid," Butch called, trotting after Lou.

"No!" Lou shouted, spinning around to face Butch. "They can't do this!"

"As long as the cats don't get the formula, we'll have done our job."

"But they're going to kill them!" Lou said.

The lab's face hardened.

"We have our orders. They'll be here for his work in an hour."

"But—"

"Look, kid. I'm sorry it's played out like this, but *it's over!*"

Lou turned and raced into the Brody house. He threw himself onto the kitchen linoleum and sobbed.

"Scott!" he cried. "Mrs. Brody! Ohhhhh!"

After he was all cried out, Lou sat with his chin on his paws, thinking.

And suddenly it came to him.

A solution.

With a growl of determination, Lou reached up and unbuckled his collar. Then he headed to the lab.

An hour later, Lou, pulling a heavy red trailer, reached the Ninth Street Bridge. He paused and peeked back at his heavy load. It was all there – every bit of Professor Brody's allergy research. Lou had strained every muscle in his body to haul it through the streets to the evil Persian's meeting place.

The puppy gazed out at the horizon. The sun was rising. It was almost dawn, just as the Persian had instructed.

Sighing, Lou gripped the trailer's handle in his teeth and resumed his journey. He was almost at the centre of the bridge. Only a few feet more . . .

"Bark! Bark! Barkbarkbarkbark!"

Lou dropped the trailer handle and spun around.

It was Butch! He was sprinting towards Lou, leaping over potholes, splashing through puddles, bypassing all fire hydrants. In an instant, he reached Lou's side.

"What the heck are you doing?!" Butch bellowed.

Lou crossed his paws over his chest and turned his back on the old lab.

Butch growled long and low.

"Get away from the trailer, kid," he ordered. "If HQ finds out about this, I'm finished."

He stepped over to the trailer, but Lou spun around.

"GRRRRRRRR!" he growled.

"Lou," Butch said. He was surprised.

"What about man's best friend?" the puppy demanded. "History 101, remember?"

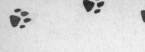

"Okay," Butch rumbled. "Well, here's lesson number two: We protect them, we work for them, we tolerate that stupid 'Butchie, Butchie' baby talk. And for what? So when they go off to college, they can stick you with some old lady who can't throw a ball without so much as breaking a hip!"

"Is that what happened to you?!" Lou barked. "You're blaming the whole world for what *one boy* did to you?"

"Ooooh," Butch growled. He looked like he was going to attack when a jolt knocked him off balance.

"Huh?" he said, looking around.

Suddenly the bridge began to split in two.

"Butch!" Lou cried. He looked around wildly as the bridge – the *drawbridge* – began to rise into the air.

"The trailer!" Butch howled.

Lou spun around in time to see the trailer sliding away. It was thundering down the other side of the rising bridge. And the gap was getting wider with each passing second.

Lou and Butch gave each other a quick look.

"One . . . two . . ." Butch counted.

"Three!" Lou yelped.

The dogs took a flying leap across the gap.

Whomp!

They made it! Well, just barely. Lou's hind legs flailed through the air as he struggled to get a grip on the metal beams beneath the bridge. With a few grunts and groans, he and Butch got a pawhold and peeked over the edge of the still-rising bridge.

Lou gasped.

There at the bottom of the bridge – right next to the trailer full of Professor Brody's research – was the Persian! A long, shiny limousine was parked behind him. The evil cat grinned up at the helpless dogs.

"Hello, my foolish foes," he snarled. "I told you I would beat you. Now, time to kill the shaved apes you called the Brodys!"

"No!" Lou cried. "You have the formula! Go ahead and use it to cure cat allergies or whatever, but let them go."

"Stupid canine," the Persian sneered, peering at a test tube of precious coloured liquid. "Do you think I would go to all this trouble just to make humans like kitties more? I'm afraid not."

Lou heard Butch gulp.

"You see," the Persian meowed, "an allergy is just like any disease. To find the cure, you must first produce the disease in its purest form. So, somewhere in here is the substance that *makes humans allergic to dogs.*"

Butch gasped.

"That's been your plan all along," he barked. "To get rid of dogs . . ."

"Yes!" the Persian screamed, and laughed. "I'll make the world violently allergic to your wretched kind. And when you're all hated and despised by those you protect, the earth will be mine for the conquering!"

With that, Calico and the Persian's other feline flunkies gathered up Professor Brody's research and

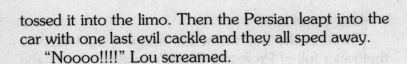

tossed it into the limo. Then the Persian leapt into the car with one last evil cackle and they all sped away.

"Noooo!!!!" Lou screamed.

Chapter Thirteen

Butch didn't speak to Lou the whole walk home. Not that Lou really wanted to talk. He was too shaken, too scared, to even try to get back on Butch's good side.

When they got back to the Brodys' house, Butch disappeared through the plank fence. Lou slumped into the living room.

If only I could find some way . . . he thought. Suddenly his eye fell on the VCR. The Persian's video! Maybe there was a clue on the tape!

Lou galloped outside to the kennel to fetch the video. He popped it into the VCR and began watching the Persian's smarmy speech over and over and over.

"You have until dawn to comply," the Persian said at the message's end. "Ah-ha-ha-ha-*screeeeee*."

Lou rewound. He played the scene again, peering at the screen, searching, searching . . .

"C'mon, you." It was Butch, standing in the living room door. "Time to face the music."

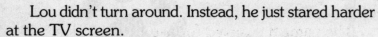

Lou didn't turn around. Instead, he just stared harder at the TV screen.

"No," he insisted. "I know I can find a clue here."

"Don't you think you've done enough?" Butch asked. "We'll be lucky if we get off with a court-martial."

The Persian finished his evil cackle and the screen went blue. The tape was still playing, but there was nothing left to watch.

Lou turned to Butch.

"They're gonna die, and it's all my fault."

"Nobody wins in this one, kid. Now c'mon."

Lou nodded sadly and plodded towards the door.

"Happy birthday to you . . ."

Huh? Lou and Butch both whirled around. Who was singing?

"Happy birthday to you!"

"It's the tape!" Lou yelled, scampering to the TV. The blue screen had been replaced by a grainy, shaky home movie.

"The Persian must have taped over this," Butch exclaimed.

"Wow, that guy's really old!" Lou said. He was staring at a yellow-faced, wrinkly old man in a hospital bed. The man wore a cardboard birthday hat, but he didn't seem to be enjoying his celebration. In fact, he was staring into space, completely out of it.

Then a lady appeared. She must have been the one singing. She wore a black maid's dress with a frilly white apron, and she held an enormous birthday cake.

" 'HAPPY 104TH BIRTHDAY, MR. MASON,' " Butch read

on the cake.

The camera swerved to take in a scowling white fluffy cat. A cat in a birthday hat and satin clown suit. A cat with a demonic, squashy face.

Lou and Butch gaped at each other. The Persian!

"Hooray," said the maid. "Meeester Teeenkles, you can help Mr. Mason blow out the candles!"

"Oh, wow," Lou giggled. Then he pointed at the top of the screen. "*Look!*"

A banner was hanging behind the old man's hospital bed.

"It says, 'HAPPY BIRTHDAY FROM ALL YOUR EMPLOYEES AT MASON TREE FLOCKING, INC.,'" Butch read.

"And look at that Christmas tree on the banner," Lou said excitedly. "It's just like that stationery they found in the Russian blue. Butch . . ."

"I know just what you're thinking," the lab said. "But no way, kid. I told you – this is over our heads."

"But you could save your job," Lou protested. "And . . . the world."

Butch scowled and avoided Lou's pleading gaze.

"C'mon, Butch, they're my family," the puppy begged. "Don't blame them for what your boy did to you."

Butch hung his head for a moment. Lou peered at his boss. Was that determination he saw glinting in Butch's eye? Or . . . a tear? More importantly, what was Butch gonna do?

* * *

Calico paced along the window of Mr. Mason's office, feeling . . . powerful. He looked around and sighed happily.

In the corner, Mr. Mason was slumped in his wheelchair.

Down below, an army of cats was hard at work, modifying the flocking machines to carry out Mr. Tinkles's diabolical scheme.

Huddled on the floor, blindfolded and bound, the Brodys trembled with fear.

And Calico was guarding them all.

"Don't be scared, Scotty," Mrs. Brody said shrilly. "Everything's going to be okay."

"I'm not scared, Mom. I'm fine."

Oh-ho, Calico thought. That's what you think!

"It's all right to be scared," Mrs. Brody squeaked. "It's perfectly natural. We'll be okay."

"Mom. I'm not scared. Really."

"I know you're trying to a big, brave man," his mother insisted. "But it's gonna be okay."

"Mom . . ."

"Darn it, Scotty," she screamed. "*Don't be scared. I'm your rock!*"

"Carolyn," the professor said, "please, calm down. We're all scared."

"*I'm not scared,*" Mrs. Brody screamed again. "*Scotty is.*"

"Okay," the boy quavered, "*now* I'm scared."

The Manx entered the room. Behind him stalked Mr. Tinkles, clutching a glass jar of pillowy fake snow.

"Hello, Professor Brody," the Persian said. "Sorry to keep you waiting, but we had a few tests to run."

"Who are you?" Professor Brody asked. He was tilting his head painfully, trying to peek from beneath his blindfold.

"Is this about my work?" the man demanded. "You're from a rival pharmaceutical company, trying to steal my—"

"Pharmaceutical company?" Mr. Tinkles said with a dry laugh. "I'm afraid you misunderstand me, Professor."

Then he nodded to Calico. Oooh, this is gonna be good, Calico thought as he slunk behind Professor Brody and untied his blindfold.

The man blinked hard. He looked wildly around the room. But, of course, all he saw were a few cats, staring at him with wry smiles.

"Show your face," the professor yelled. "Coward!"

Meanwhile, Calico untied Mrs. Brody's blindfold and the boy's, too.

"You can't hide forever," Professor Brody called.

And that was when Mr. Tinkles made his move. He hopped onto the professor's lap, looked deep into the man's confused brown eyes, and spoke.

"Oh, I've nothing to hide," he announced.

"*AAAAIIIIIIIIIGGGGHHHH!*"

It was Mrs. Brody. She's freakin', Calico thought with glee.

"Cooool!" Scott said.

"*AAAAIIIGGGHHH!*" Mrs. Brody continued.

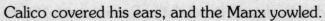

Calico covered his ears, and the Manx yowled.

"Will someone please shut her up?" Mr. Tinkles screeched. "I have an ingenious test to perform!"

Scott wasn't freaked at all, Calico noticed with disappointment. In fact, he was fascinated.

"Are you, like, mutants or something?" he asked Mr. Tinkles breathlessly. "'Cause I read this comic book whe—"

"'Cause I read this comic book,'" Mr. Tinkles simpered. Then he spat. "You make me sick!"

"*AAAAAAIIIIIIGGGGGGHHHH,*" screamed Mrs. Brody.

"Carolyn!" Professor Brody said. "Calm down! I'm sure these things are just part of some ill-conceived experiment gone awry, and . . ."

The professor gazed at his screeching wife with increasing alarm.

"*Stop screaming, Carolyn! You're turning blue!*"

With that, Mrs. Brody's oxygen ran out. She stopped screaming. In fact, she fainted.

"It's about time," Mr. Tinkles said, rolling his eyes and hopping over Mrs. Brody's feet. "Now . . ."

Mr. Tinkles looked at the three humans and settled for . . . Scott. He padded up to the boy with a handful of fake snow.

"What . . . what is that?" Professor Brody asked.

The snow still poised on his palm, Mr. Tinkles turned to the professor. A smile slowly squinched his squashy face.

"You see, my quote-unquote *master's* fake snow is

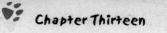

the perfect medium for carrying your 'disease'," he said. "Thereby breaking the bond between a boy and his dog!"

Before Scott could duck, the Persian blew a cloud of the snow into his face. Scott shook his head and held his breath. Mr. Tinkles laughed and flicked his fluffy tail beneath the boy's nose.

"*Hunh!*" the boy gasped, sucking in a gust of air. Immediately, the Manx stepped forward and thrust a small cage into Scott's face. Inside the cage was a tiny chihuahua, yapping and snarling.

Calico watched Scott eye the nasty little cur. And then he gasped with excitement as the boy's nose began to twitch. And twitter. And drip.

"*Aaaachooo!*" Scott sneezed.

"Ha!" Mr. Tinkles screeched. "Success!"

He pointed at the Manx.

"Downstairs," he ordered.

"And as for you," Mr. Tinkles said to the trembling Brodys (for the stunned Mrs. Brody had just woken up), "I have a special gift."

Leaping onto Mr. Mason's desk, he opened a wooden box. And from the box, he began to pull – a glinting pistol!

Mr. Tinkles gripped the butt of the gun and tugged.

"Ooof!"

He tugged some more.

"*Urgh!*"

He turned his venomous yellow eyes upon Calico.

"You couldn't have purchased a cat-sized gun,

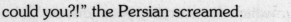

could you?!" the Persian screamed.

"Boss—" Calico protested.

But it was too late. Mr. Tinkles flung the pistol at Calico in rage.

The gun hit the floor and went off. *Bang!*

Then the pistol bounced onto the battery pack of Mr. Mason's wheelchair and went off again. *Ker-ching!*

"Ack!" the Brodys screamed as the bullet slammed into a metal garbage can.

It ricocheted! *Ker-chung!*

The slug hit a metal file cabinet and rebounded again. *Ker-thunk!*

Finally, the bullet pierced the plastic water cooler – and stopped.

"Phew," Calico sighed as a harmless stream of water flowed out of the cooler. At least, it seemed harmless. Until it splashed onto a nearby wall socket. *Bzzzztttt.*

The socket sputtered and smoked. And then it sparked, catching a nearby window curtain and igniting it.

"Eeeek!" Mr. Tinkles squealed. "Er . . . I mean . . . I'm so clever. Gun, fire, who cares? Either way, you all *die!*"

The Brodys stared after the evil cat as he quickly stalked through the office door. Calico was on his heels when the Persian spun around and held out a paw.

"I want you to stay here."

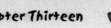

"Uh, why, Boss?"

"Because I hate you!" Mr. Tinkles screamed. Then he slammed the office door and locked it.

Calico hurled himself at the door.

"Noooooo!"

Meanwhile, Lou and Butch were peering through a window of Mason Tree Flocking, Inc. They saw two helmeted cats guarding the doorway that led to the factory floor.

Lou looked at Butch and grinned. This was it! Only an hour earlier, Butch had consented to a rescue mission. And now they'd found the cats!

Butch tossed a rope through the window and began to abseil silently down the inside wall. Lou followed.

Suddenly he heard a feline hiss. They'd been spotted!

In a flash, Butch pulled a black canister from his collar. He tossed it down to the cats.

"Hey!" they shouted. "Hey! *Heeeeeyyyy!*"

As the canister spewed a yellow mist, the cats began to giggle and stagger.

But Lou and Butch dropped into the room stone sober.

"What is that stuff?" Lou asked.

"Concentrated catnip," Butch explained. As the guards collapsed, Butch nudged the factory door open.

"Now we just need to figure out how they're gonna spread the allergen."

Butch motioned Lou through the door. The puppy and the lab scurried over to hide behind some giant cans labelled FLOCKING COMPOUND – FLAMMABLE.

Lou peeked around the can and gasped.

The factory was overrun by cats – cats loading fake snow into giant sprayers; cats hovering over some kind of map; cats barking orders at other cats. And then Lou saw some other animals, animals who were definitely *not* cats.

"Uh, Butch," he quavered. "I think I know how they're gonna spread the allergy."

Butch followed Lou's gaze.

"Son of my mom!" he gasped.

"And look!" Lou pointed.

High over the dogs' heads, the evil cat that they now knew as Mr. Tinkles was stalking down a, well, catwalk. Haughtily, he stepped onto a crane, which lowered him to the factory floor. When the Persian lifted a megaphone to his face his psychotic screech echoed through the factory.

"In just hours, every human in the world will be allergic to dogs," he announced.

"*Mrowr, mrowr, mrowr,*" the cats cheered.

"But such a mammoth plot requires brothers in arms," Mr. Tinkles continued. "And this is where my genius truly comes to pass. For I have chosen a comrade that can invade every home in the world because *it is already in every home in the world.*"

He pointed a fluffy paw at the conveyer belts.

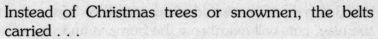

Instead of Christmas trees or snowmen, the belts carried . . .

"Mice! The unlikeliest of allies. Thousands of you. Each one covered with concentrated dog allergy."

Thousands of tiny rodents whizzed into the flocking machine. As they entered, they were grey or brown or speckled. But when they emerged, every mouse was white – covered in fake snow.

Soon Mr. Tinkles was herding great hordes of white mice towards a tall velvet curtain. He stood before the twittering animals, his back arched and his fur expanded to full fluffiness.

"I am sure you are all asking, 'What comes next? How can he possibly spread the allergy to the world?'"

The Persian whipped a little black book from behind his back. Licking a footpad, he began thumbing through it.

"So, if you will open your World Domination pamphlets to page three," he said, "I will show you."

Lou shook his head in disbelief as every cat and mouse in the room began thumbing through their own little black books.

"You are to enter into the sewers," Mr. Tinkles announced. "Using the maps provided in Appendix B, you will make your way across the nation. Half of you will infiltrate homes – infecting every human in sight – while the other half – turn the page . . ."

A great rustling of pages filled the room.

"While the other half," Mr. Tinkles continued, "will stow away on planes, boats, and dirigibles to infect

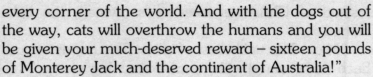

every corner of the world. And with the dogs out of the way, cats will overthrow the humans and you will be given your much-deserved reward – sixteen pounds of Monterey Jack and the continent of Australia!"

"*Squeak, squeak, squeak,*" the mice cheered.

"Oh, no!" Butch groaned.

"*Open the sewer hatch,*" Mr. Tinkles commanded. The velvet curtain tumbled to the floor, revealing an enormous round metal door. Two cats tugged on the handle. Slowly the door swung open. Somewhere drums began playing military march music.

"*MROWR!*" the cats roared triumphantly.

The mice formed straight lines and began to march toward the sewer hatch.

"The fate of the world is in your little pink paws," Mr. Tinkles yelled through his megaphone. "So go! To victory!"

Chapter Fourteen

*T*he mice marched.

The cats cheered.

Mr. Tinkles celebrated his triumph.

And that was when Butch gave Lou a wink.

"Ready?" he asked.

"Ready!" Lou barked. Together they pushed.

CLANG! CLUNK! CRASH!

"Squeak! Mrowr! Aaaaaaaaaaaahhhh!"

Cats and mice scattered as a dozen enormous barrels of fake snow began tumbling onto the factory floor. The barrels careered into the flocking machines, smashing them open like walnuts. Snow spewed everywhere. And then the barrels rolled on, crashing into the sewer hatch.

A shrill sound filled the air.

Beeeep. Beeep. Beeeep.

It was a forklift, chugging through the drifts of fake snow. And out of the vehicle's cab rumbled the voice of a grizzled labrador retriever.

"Surrender, cats," Butch bellowed. "You're finished."

"Dogs! Kill them!" Mr. Tinkles screeched at his cat flunkies. Then he pointed at the cowering crew of mice.

"Mice! Go!" he ordered.

As the mice scrambled to get back into marching formation, a group of muscled cat guards bounded over to the forklift. When they threw open the door of the cab, however, they saw no dog at all – only a brick on the accelerator and a red collar with a silver button.

"Curiosity killed the cat!" the collar said. Then a puff of concentrated catnip surged into the air. In an instant, Mr. Tinkles's best goons collapsed onto the floor, giggling helplessly. The forklift crashed into the wall with a crunch.

"Ignore it, mice," Mr. Tinkles screeched. "Into the hatch. Into the hatch!"

That's my cue, Lou thought.

"Not so fast!" he yelled. He leaped out from behind the fallen barrels to block the sewer door. Butch was right behind him. Before one snow-dusted mouse could make it into the tunnel, the dogs pushed the door closed.

"Get them!" Mr. Tinkles screamed. A new batch of kitty goons leaped to face Lou and Butch. But the dogs were ready for them. Each crouched in kung fu fighting stance.

"You!" Lou yelled, pointing at Mr. Tinkles above the goons' heads. "Where's my family?!"

Ba-BOOM!

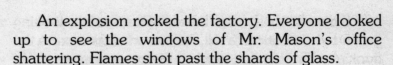

An explosion rocked the factory. Everyone looked up to see the windows of Mr. Mason's office shattering. Flames shot past the shards of glass.

"*AAAAIIIIIGGGGGGHHHH!*" a woman screamed.

"Mrs. Brody!" Lou gasped.

"Oh," Mr. Tinkles said with mock concern. "I wonder if they're up there."

Lou shot Butch a desperate look.

"I got this," Butch said as ten cats struck ninja poses before them. "You go."

"But you can't do this alone!" Lou protested.

"He's not alone."

The dogs whirled around to see a silvery weimaraner standing near the sewer hatch. Ivy! And not just Ivy – Ivy with a fire hose.

"Bath time," she announced. Then she hit the cats and mice with a pelting spray.

"*Mrrrrroooowwwrr,*" cried the cats, dashing away from the hated jets of water.

"*Squeeeeeaaaaak,*" squealed the mice as the allergy-laced flocking was blasted from their backs.

Lou had to grin as he raced across the factory floor. He gritted his teeth and headed for Mr. Mason's office.

Dodging shooting flames, he ran up Mr. Tinkles's crane to the catwalk and dashed into the office's reception area.

"*Aaaaaahhh!*"

There was Mrs. Brody again! Lou had to get in there! But how? He jumped up and tried to twist the

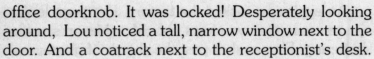

office doorknob. It was locked! Desperately looking around, Lou noticed a tall, narrow window next to the door. And a coatrack next to the receptionist's desk.

Training or no training, Lou knew what to do. Using a surge of super dog strength, he gripped the coatrack in his teeth.

"*Hiiiii-yah!*" he screamed as he flung the rack at the window. The glass shattered and flames shot out of the office. But the puppy was undaunted.

"*Woof, woof!*" he barked.

"Lou? Lou!" called a voice inside the office. It was Scott!

Lou backed up and took a running leap. He vaulted over the shooting flames and into the half-burned office. They were all there – Professor Brody, Mrs. Brody, and Scott! That old man, Mr. Mason, was there, too. And so was that evil calico cat!

"I told you he wasn't a loser!" Mrs. Brody cried.

"We're saved!" Calico exclaimed. "Gotta go!"

Without a look back, the cat bolted through the broken window. Lou growled and ran over to Mrs. Brody to unknot the ropes on her hands. Quickly, she and Lou both freed Scott and Professor Brody. Just in the nick of time, too. Smoke was filling the office and the flames were closing in.

Scott scooped Lou into his arms.

"How'd you find us?" the boy whispered to the puppy. "Can you talk, too?"

Lou hesitated just long enough for Scott to let out a huge sneeze.

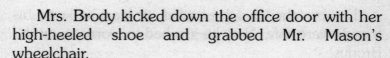

Mrs. Brody kicked down the office door with her high-heeled shoe and grabbed Mr. Mason's wheelchair.

"Move your butts, boys!" she hollered. They all bolted out of the room. As Scott carried Lou into the reception area, the puppy looked over the boy's shoulder to see the smouldering office ceiling cave in. Whew!

He twisted around to see yet another obstacle. The door to the reception area was blocked by a wall of fire.

"What do we do?" Mrs. Brody wailed.

"We could improvise a simple retardant," Professor Brody suggested, "with some chalk, a quart of sodium silicate fifty, and a—"

It looked like Mrs. Brody was about to give her husband a swat when the most unlikely of heroes dropped through a hatch in the ceiling. It was the calico cat!

"This way!" he yelled. He led the family through a cloud of smoke to a window that led to the rickety network of catwalks. The main walkway carried them out over the factory floor. Scott put Lou down, and the puppy peeked over the catwalk's edge. He could see Butch and Ivy! The dogs were holding the fire hose in their jaws. But the water coming from the hose was waning to a trickle. Lou saw Butch say something to Ivy and point at the growing flames. Then both dogs raced for the exit with a throng of screaming mice and cats.

Lou breathed a sigh of relief. At least he knew his friends were safe. Now he just had to worry about the Brodys!

"C'mon," the calico called. He ran to the other end of the walkway and paused to beckon to the humans and Lou. They had just begun to follow when –

CRASH!

An enormous hook slammed into the catwalk. It ripped a chunk out of the metal platform, making it impossible for the Brodys to go any farther. Lou gasped and gaped down at the factory floor.

Mr. Tinkles was behind the wheel of the crane. Wildly, he swung its huge mechanical arm – and the hook that hung from it.

"Ha-ha!" he cackled through his megaphone. "Ah-ha-ha-*screeeeee!*"

"Ow!" Scott said, putting his fingers in his ears. "Gnarly feedback on that megaphone."

The evil Persian banged on the bullhorn.

"How does this work . . . oh. Okay . . . Ah-ha-ha-*screeeee*. Darn! Prepare to d-*screeeeeeeee*. Aigh!"

The cat was even more enraged now. He tossed the megaphone to the floor, pointed at the Brodys, and swiped a claw across his throat.

Yeah, we get it, Lou thought grimly. Prepare to die.

The Persian swung the hook back for another strike. Lou could see the calico on the other side of the factory, fleeing for his life. But he and the Brodys had

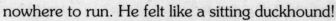 

nowhere to run. He felt like a sitting duckhound!

"Turn around," Professor Brody yelled. "Let's go back!"

CRASH!

The hook collided with the catwalk again and their path of escape crumpled before their eyes. Mr. Tinkles unleashed another evil cackle.

Desperately, Lou turned to his right. There was another catwalk. But where did it lead? He squinted through the smoke. . . . Ah-ha!

"*Arf, arf, arf!*" he called to his family. They looked down at him. He ran down the catwalk, then turned to look back at them.

"I think he's trying to tell us something!" Professor Brody said.

"*Follow him!*" Mrs. Brody snapped.

Pushing Mr. Mason in his chair, Mrs. Brody charged after Lou with Scott and Professor Brody on her heels. Lou ran across a platform filled with flaming snowmen and sparkly Christmas wreaths. And then he came to an enormous fan. Its huge, razor-sharp blades whirled around wildly. But through the blades, Lou could see sunlight. This was their way outside!

"We can't go through there!" Mrs. Brody wailed, falling against the catwalk banister.

"We can if we can turn it off," Professor Brody retorted. He crouched down and peered through the fan. Then he pointed a long, skinny finger at a big red button on the wall just beyond the fan.

"There!"

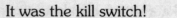

It was the kill switch!

"Find something to throw at it!" the professor called.

CRASH!

Lou whirled around. The enormous hook had smashed away another section of the walkway. And it was only yards behind them!

"Ah-ha-ha-ha," Mr. Tinkles cackled from down below. The hook began to swing back for another blow. That was when Lou spotted something teetering at the end of the crushed catwalk. A plastic snowman head! It was slightly charred and missing its *eyes*, but that didn't matter. What *did* matter was that the plastic head was just about the size of – a soccer ball!

"*Arf!*" Lou yelped. He nosed the head down the catwalk and pushed it onto Scott's toe. The boy looked down at Lou with wide eyes.

"*Woof!*" Lou barked.

Scott gritted his teeth.

"Outta the way," he announced. He backed up and squinted at the ball.

"Scotty," Mrs. Brody said nervously, "I know you're a good player and all, even though your father never made it to your tryouts, but—"

"Carolyn, he can do it," Professor Brody interrupted. He smiled at Scott. "I know he can."

Scott smiled back. He took a deep breath and began running. He kicked the snowman head. It soared through the air and – missed. By a country mile. The head bounced off the fan and hit

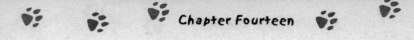

Professor Brody in the stomach.

Mrs. Brody glared at her husband.

"I begged you to practise with him!"

CRASH!

There was the hook again! Now they only had a few feet of catwalk left to stand on. Mr. Tinkles was laughing madly down below.

"*Arf, arf!*" Lou barked, gazing anxiously as Scott.

Professor Brody stared at the ball. Then he stared at the fan. Then he stared at Scott's big trainer.

"Fourteen degrees," he announced. "You're off by fourteen degrees."

"Yeah, I miss it every time," Scott scowled.

The professor grabbed the snowman head and planted it on the catwalk. Doing some quick, mental calculations, he pointed at a spot on the head.

"Just kick it here," he told his son.

Scott bit his lip, but Professor Brody nodded, full of confidence.

Scott took another deep breath. He ran at the snowman's head and kicked hard – the head shot right through the fan and landed on the big red kill switch with a *thwack*! Instantly, the fan whirred to a halt!

"That's my boy!" Professor Brody cried. "Let's go!"

Lou looked over his shoulder. The hook was arcing backwards in the air. The evil Persian was going for one more lethal blow!

"*Arf, arf, arf,*" he barked in warning.

Mrs. Brody shoved Mr. Mason's chair between the

fan blades and skittered through behind him. Finally she reached back to help Scott through the blades. Just Professor Brody was left . . .

But the hook was only a few feet away! Lou could hear it whistling through the air. By the time Scott made it through the fan, the professor had run out of time! Unless . . .

Lou leaped. He jumped with every bit of power left in his body. And he hit Professor Brody square in the back.

"Ooof," the man grunted. The puppy's force vaulted him through the fan blades and he somersaulted to safety.

But Lou wasn't so lucky. The hook bashed him right in the gut!

"*Arp!*" he yelped, feeling a sharp pain in his belly. He landed on the other side of the fan. When he looked up, he saw that the hook was lying next to him.

"*Ah-ha-ha-ha,*" Mr. Tinkles cackled. The hook started to pull away. The dastardly Persian was pulling it back to level one more blow!

But Lou wasn't about to let that happen!

With a grown-up growl, he leaped for the kill switch and smashed it with his paw. The fan began whirling, catching the hook in its blades. That meant the hook's cable was drawn into the fan as well!

Peering through the blades, Lou could see Mr. Tinkles struggling inside the cab of the crane as he was dragged forwards by the whirling fan. The cat screeched in rage, then burst into psychotic laughter.

Grabbing his bullhorn, the Persian screamed at his puppy nemesis.

"Do you think you have won? I sh-*screeeeee*. Darn it!"

Lou started to laugh at the pathetic villain. But as the first giggle escaped his lips, the hook wrenched the fan out of the wall, and the catwalk Lou was standing on went with it!

Tangled in fan blades, duct work, and cables, Lou plummeted towards the factory floor. He gasped as the cement floor raced up at him and he heard a voice echo through the factory. It was a rumbly, familiar voice – Butch!

"Loooouuu!" the lab bellowed.

Ba-BOOOOMMM!

Lou felt a fireball shake the factory. And then everything went black!

Chapter Fifteen

The calico was standing paw-cuffed in front of the flaming flocking factory. Sam and Peek were reading him his rights.

"I mean, I like dogs," Calico tried to tell them. "I like people. But Mr. Tinkles was my only friend. Or so I thought!"

Ba-BOOOOM!

An enormous explosion rocked the factory. Calico looked around. The Brodys were cowering behind Mr. Mason's limousine. The kid was crying for his puppy. Mr. Mason, looking more stunned than ever, was parked in his wheelchair on the driveway. And there were mice everywhere.

Ooooh, this is bad, Calico thought nervously. Better lay it on thick! He looked at Sam and announced, "My therapist says I might be a dog trapped in a cat's body . . ."

"Tell it to the judge," Sam panted. He was leading the cat to the HQ Van when something made him stop.

"Peek!" Sam huffed. "Lookit! It's Butch and Lou."

Calico and his captors gaped as the grizzled old lab bounded out of the burning factory. His fur was charred and blackened. From his teeth hung the equally scorched Lou. The puppy was completely limp.

The lab laid Lou on the cement and nudged him with his nose.

"Kid – kid? We did it!" he implored. "Kid?"

The puppy lay still, his eyes clamped shut. He didn't move a muscle.

"We saved them," Butch barked. He sounded desperate. Calico almost felt sorry for him. "Just like you said. You were right. And you were right about me. . . . Kid? Lou? Oh, no!"

"Lou?!"

That was the boy. He stumbled away from his stricken parents and ran to his dog. With tears welling up in his eyes, he picked up the drooping puppy.

"Lou . . . Lou," he whimpered.

Awww, there's only so much a cat can take, Calico thought, swiping at his watering eyes.

"*Cough.*"

Huh?

"*Cough-cough.*"

It was Lou! He was alive! Weak and groaning, but alive!

"You made it!" Scott cried. "*Achoo!* Mom, Dad! He's alive! *Achoo!* Lou's alive!"

The Brodys all exclaimed with surprise and joy.

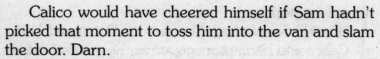

Calico would have cheered himself if Sam hadn't picked that moment to toss him into the van and slam the door. Darn.

Lou blinked blearily. He looked around, confused. Where was he?

He saw Butch grinning down at him. And then he was being scooped up into Scott's arms. His boy was crying with joy while Professor and Mrs. Brody tousled his ears happily. And Ivy was there, too. Everyone was okay, Lou realized. They'd saved the formula and his family! And most important, they'd defeated the evil Mr. Tin—

"Nine lives," meowed a smoke-charred voice.

Lou gasped and twisted in Scott's arms. It was the evil Persian! He was crouched behind Mr. Mason's wheelchair. Most of his fur had been singed off and the few fluffy patches that remained looked a lot like – a bikini!

The sight would have been hilarious, if Mr. Tinkles hadn't been clutching his very large pistol in his paws. He was pointing it at all of them.

"Or did you forget?" Mr. Tinkles sneered. "Yes, you may have ruined my plans, defeated my cat army, and foiled my crane vengeance . . . you might have even stopped the mice and saved the humans . . . and the world . . . but I . . ."

Suddenly the Persian screamed in frustration. His yellow eyes practically spun with rage.

"Oh, I hate you so much! Die!!"

He aimed the gun and struggled to squeeze the

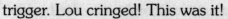

trigger. Lou cringed! This was it!

But then something dropped onto the Persian like a bag of rocks. And that something was the wrinkled, sallow hand of – Mr. Mason!

Mr. Tinkles dropped the gun and spun around. When he saw Mr. Mason's cloudy eyes staring down upon him, he yowled bloody murder.

The old man glared at his cat and uttered two very true words.

"Bad kitty."

Mr. Tinkles's face crumpled into an unrecognizable mush. His yellow eyes bulged and his charred lips quivered.

And then he unleashed a desperate scream.

"Noooooooo!"

In only a few days, Lou was totally recovered. What was more, Professor Brody was totally changed. He was even . . . sporty!

In fact, at this very moment, he was practising headers in the back yard.

"Come on, Scotty," he called. "Let's try again!"

Scott dribbled his soccer ball across the grass as Lou nipped happily at Scott's heels.

"Maybe we should stop," Scott said to his dad. "Your head's all red . . ."

"Oh, no!" Professor Brody insisted. "I can get it right."

"Okay," Scott said. He lobbed the ball to his dad. Professor Brody sprang into the air and gave it a

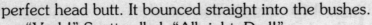
perfect head butt. It bounced straight into the bushes.

"Yeah!" Scott yelled. "All right, Dad!"

Lou barked in approval and trotted to the shrubs to get the ball. As he ducked into the leaves, he heard a familiar rumbly voice.

"Hey, kid."

"Butch!" Lou said, smiling at his boss. The old lab was poking his head through the fence panel.

"Everything go okay at HQ?" Lou asked.

"I have them eating out of my paw," Butch said with a smile. "How're things here?"

"Great!" Lou said. "Wanna play some ball?"

"Nah, I've got to get back to work."

"Oh," Lou said, nodding seriously.

"Well, actually . . ." Butch said, looking sheepish, "I've gotta get home. Mrs. Calvert likes me and Ivy to watch Thursday night Must See TV with her."

Lou gaped at Butch and tried to suppress his giggles.

"What?!" Butch growled. "So the old lady's grown on me. Got a problem with that?"

"Sir, no, sir!"

"Good!" Butch said. "Out!"

And he was gone.

So was the calico cat. Gone from kitty prison, that is.

"Heh-heh-heh-heh," he snickered from his hiding place in the veterinarian's office. "No jail can hold Calico."

Then he clamped his mouth shut. It was starting. He peeked out of his hiding place with squinty eyes.

"You have been a very bad kitty," Calico heard a voice say. It was the silly, Italian-accented voice of none other than Sophie the maid.

She bustled into the vet's and peered into the cat carrier in her hand. Inside, Mr. Tinkles was scowling in prison-issue black-and-white stripes.

"Yes, very bad, Meeester Teeenkles!" Sophie said. "Mr. Mason say he know just how to calm you down."

The maid flashed a grin. A slightly sinister grin. And she scissored two fingers back and forth.

"Sneep-sneep!" she cackled.

Mr. Tinkles let loose a high-pitched screech as Sophie planted the cat carrier on the vet's counter. She smiled at the nurse sitting behind the desk and said, "Yes, one o'clock sneep-sneep and pedicure for a Meeester Teeenkles."

The nurse nodded silently.

"He is a verrrrry bad kitty," Sophie prattled on. "He try to take over the world."

The nurse nodded some more. Then she nodded harder. Until finally her bobbling head nodded right off of her neck!

"*Ai-yeeeeee!*" Sophie screamed. Her eyes bulged as a parade of cats climbed out of the "nurse". First Calico leaped out. Then the Manx, the Havana brown, and the whole crew followed. Calico leaped over to Mr. Tinkles's cat carrier and unlatched the door, setting his devious leader free.

The cats were back in business.

But so were the dogs. A few minutes later, on the other side of town, Lou's collar crackled to life. The puppy dived into the bushes to answer his agent call to arms.

"Lou!" It was Butch. "We got a problem!"

"Mission number two, here I come!"